CW01593987

Stephen U'Ren was raised in Arizona by two public school teachers, both of whom read whenever possible and passed the habit on to their four children. Mr. U'Ren attended Northern Arizona University and law at the University of Arizona. He worked in Juneau, Alaska and then in El Mirage Arizona followed by a solo practice until retirement allowed more handball, seasons as a volunteer ranger at Yellowstone National Park and hiking in Grand Canyon while writing in Arizona and Montana. Mr. U'Ren is married with two adult children and four grandchildren.

I would like to dedicate this set of short stories to my high school English teacher who strongly encouraged me and many others to read and read again, which many of us did.

Stephen U'Ren

A Soldier's Prerogative and Other Short Stories

Austin Macauley Publishers®
London * Cambridge * New York * Sharjah

Copyright © Stephen U'Ren 2025

All rights reserved. No part of this publication may be reproduced, distributed, or transmitted in any form or by any means, including photocopying, recording, or other electronic or mechanical methods, without the prior written permission of the publisher, except in the case of brief quotations embodied in critical reviews and certain other non-commercial uses permitted by copyright law. For permission requests, write to the publisher.

Any person who commits any unauthorized act in relation to this publication may be liable to criminal prosecution and civil claims for damages.

This is a work of fiction. Names, characters, businesses, places, events, locales, and incidents are either the products of the author's imagination or used in a fictitious manner. Any resemblance to actual persons, living or dead, or actual events is purely coincidental.

Ordering Information
Quantity sales: Special discounts are available on quantity purchases by corporations, associations, and others. For details, contact the publisher at the address below.

Publisher's Cataloging-in-Publication data
U'Ren, Stephen
A Soldier's Prerogative and Other Short Stories

ISBN 9798895439920 (Paperback)
ISBN 9798895439937 (Hardback)
ISBN 9798895439944 (ePub e-book)

Library of Congress Control Number: 2025911455

www.austinmacauleyusa.com

First Published 2025
Austin Macauley Publishers LLC
40 Wall Street, 33rd Floor, Suite 3302
New York, NY 10005
USA

mail-usa@austinmacauley.com
+1 (646) 5125767

I would like to acknowledge my wife, Marcia Melton, who writes historical fiction based on the history of Montana which is used in Montana middle schools.

I would like to acknowledge my brother Chip U'Ren for deep work editing.

I would like to acknowledge Nicole Garrett who easily navigated me through the tech process that is not always easy.

"Well?" asked the French doctor. "How do you feel now?" The doctor spoke with the thick-tongued accent of a Frenchman speaking English, though his words were correct and he spoke with a smile. "Fine, I feel fine now," answered the American Army officer Lester Turner.

"Good, very good." Smiled the doctor.

"You and your people have taken good care of me. I'm appreciative." "Qui? But of course. Your country helped save us. We are very grateful!"

"But now I've missed my unit. They've shipped for home by now. I'll have to forge new orders for myself."

"Good," said the doctor again. "Very good." He never changed tone. Everything was 'very good' now. He had cured the American, and soon the American would leave, and that was all the Frenchman could care about.

He had done his job. The American could leave alive. The war was over. His patients in the hospital had infirmities other than war injuries, and not all of the beds were filled. In fact, this American was one of the new patients with a non-war-caused condition. The doctor was delighted.

"I thought I was going to die," said the soldier."

"Die?" No, captain. It was only a bad foreign virus that your body did not know how to deal with."

"Still, I thought it would kill me just when the war ended."

"No, it could not have done so, not to a strong man like you."

Despite what the French doctor now said, Captain Turner had believed that the virus would kill him. He had been convinced of it. It wasn't the type or the severity of the disease that convinced him; rather, it was the disease's timing. Not once during the war had the cry of medic been raised for the captain, nor had he seen the inside of a hospital tent for illness. Never in the course of the war had he felt the paralyzed or frozen mind that some others had experienced. And in Berlin, when the war was over, the captain still dared not tell himself that he had survived, for then there were the days of the occupation and the "cleanup" and the waiting for news announcing whether they would be transferred to the Pacific theater for more war.

When his battalion finally received their orders to sail for home was when the captain dared to tell himself that he had fought and survived. This had been his goal for all the war: to survive and to survive without being maimed in body or mind. Next to the fear of death had been the fear that the war would change him into a different man where he had no control over any decisions. Before the orders to sail came, he refused to dwell on the war's end or home or survival for fear it would make him too cautious to be 'a good soldier—so timid that he would be dangerous as an officer.'

And it was then, after the orders had permitted him to sigh in relief, that the virus struck and his mind told him that he would yet die or be maimed.

He had been very much afraid when the illness first came, more afraid than he could remember being at any time during the war, and his fear made him feel ashamed.

With the virus now cured and the captain believing it, he grew restless and wanted to leave the hospital. The doctor wanted him to stay two days longer to be certain that all was truly well with him. The doctor radiated with the luxury of being able to take his time with a patient.

Captain Turner wanted to talk. He was again certain that he would leave Europe, and he was bored.

"Doctor, the food is not good," he would say. "Can't we do better for my first civilian meal?"

"You are not a civilian yet," replied the doctor.

"I feel like one. That's enough for me right now."

"I can see that. You act like one."

"Have you been to America, Doctor?"

"No."

"Never?"

"Never. Is it so surprising?"

"No, I suppose not. You would love Minnesota."

"I love France," said the proud doctor, then adding, "And I love America for getting Germany out of France. Thank God!"

"You are content then, doctor?"

"But of course." The doctor smiled and swung his arms. "Not even all the beds in France are full of enemies. Order has returned."

"Still, there is sickness and disease, doctor."

"Ah, but not war disease. These diseases are normal, everyday maladies; healthy diseases and common ones. Even yours is very dull." The captain smiled. "Yes, you seem full of content and much relieved."

The doctor could not tell if the American officer spoke sincerely or in jest, but his response was the same. "And should I be? Not every case is life or death now. There are no more weeks of total demand on all of my talent and judgment and ability. Some responsibility has been lifted. Not every young woman and man has a sex illness—I don't see so many with lost arms or legs."

"Yes." Nodded the captain. "Those days are over."

"I did things I did not know could be done. Things which should not be done in my profession, and I never want to have to do them again."

The captain nodded. This was something he understood. No, less than the doctor, and perhaps more, he had been subject to the demands and responsibilities of which the good doctor spoke.

"Do you not also feel contentment, captain?"

"Yes, but not the kind of contentment I want. It's strange."

"I understand, captain, I truly do."

Yet, thought the captain, it could not be a full feeling until he returned full circle to Minnesota, to where he started the journey. Then, in the farming country, when the fall deer hunts and later the duck hunts began and the meals were regular and hot and beds had sheets and work was stable and decisions unimportant and responsibilities minor, did the captain believe he would feel the full contentment of a return to normal?

Captain Turner left the hospital on a late September morning when the air was just beginning to tell that winter would come. The doctor walked the American to the door. They shook hands and embraced.

Captain Turner was tall and light and young. The doctor was short and not so young.

From the hospital, the captain commandeered a warrant officer with a jeep and located administrative headquarters for an American battalion. Though he knew none of the soldiers or officers who staffed the headquarters, he was able to make their friendship quickly. Without difficulty, Captain Turner talked the officer of the day into giving him blank orders upon which he could forge himself onto the next ship sailing for the States. Forgery would save at least thirty days but risk nothing; forgery was not alien to the captain. He had forged military orders before, when time and the battlefield did not permit him to obtain authorized signatures for what had to be done. Since the captain did not abuse the violation, nothing was ever said by superior officers, for they too knew what had to be done. Only once had Captain Turner heard of disciplinary action being taken against an officer for forgery, but that time the decision, which had been formalized by forgery, had turned to disaster. If one forged, knew the captain, one had to be right.

"What's the next ship sailing for the States?" asked a sergeant. "It's the York, sir."

"When does the York sail, Sergeant?"

"Two days, sir, 0200 on the 24th, sir."

"Good. Thank you, Sergeant. Now I need to find a ride to Marseilles. The York sails from Marseilles, doesn't it?

"Yes, sir, it does. Luck is with you now. Private Williams is driving First Lieutenant Myers down to Marseilles in the morning. I'm sure you can catch a ride."

"What time will they leave?"

"Eight o'clock, I believe."

"Banker's hours?" Laughed the captain.

The sergeant laughed also. "Regular business hours at least, captain."

"I'll be there. Inform Private Williams and Lieutenant Myers that I'll be riding with them… Is Lieutenant Myers attached to the battalion?"

"Yes. I've heard that he's been promoted, but the paperwork hasn't come through yet."

"Typical."

"The lieutenant has a very good record, sir."

"I know. I've heard of him."

The open-air jeep pulled up in front of the stone building just at eight the next morning. There was a chill in the air. Lieutenant Myers was already in the jeep with the driver. He wore his officer's issue hat and a full-length overcoat with the collar and the lapels turned up. He was tall like Captain Turner, but he had dark hair and was not as heavy as the captain. The lieutenant stepped from the jeep to introduce himself. There existed, with the lieutenant's introduction and his mannerisms, an unmistakable air of formalism or rank. He helped the captain load his bags into the jeep and then resumed his seat. Captain Turner sat in a larger seat in the back. Beyond the introduction and then a casual mention by each man that they believed they had heard of each other during the course of the war. Nothing more was said. The driver, a Black private, also helped load the captain's bags, but other than his salutation to the captain, he said nothing to either of the officers. In the back seat, the wind blew all about Captain Turner.

The morning remained fairly cold, as the French sky had clouded over with gray autumn clouds. There was little other movement on the road. Another time Captain Turner might have cursed the chill of the day and the unbroken gray of the sky, but not this morning, not when it was the morning of the first leg of his journey home.

But what of Lieutenant Myers? Wondered the captain. Certainly, no joy could be detected in him. Perhaps his joy had been spent the night before in a French bar with a French woman or both. No, thought the captain, it was more than that. There existed a somberness that could not be explained by melancholy or overindulgence of serious foul weather. But didn't the lieutenant have as much reason as he did to celebrate the war's end? He was an officer (apparently to be promoted) who had survived intact. And beyond that, he had earned himself a reputation, one the captain was vaguely familiar with by rumor. Surely, he had come to the war like the rest: inexperienced and unknown in all ways, and besides being uninjured, he was taking a reputation and proof of himself that he could not have had before coming to war. Still, a curious division dominated the jeep. Given his rank and his curiosity, it was Captain Turner's obligation to bring Lieutenant Myers into the American fold.

"You're sailing for the States on the York, lieutenant?" Asked the captain, leaning into the wind.

The lieutenant only half turned his head to reply. "Yes, captain, I am." "Where's your home, lieutenant?"

"Tennessee." The lieutenant still did not turn far enough to look his fellow officer in the eyes." It will be good to see Tennessee again after seeing the world, won't it!"

"Yes, it will; yes, it will."

"Are you married, lieutenant?"

"Yes."

"Children?"

"No, not yet."

"Your folks and family all live in Tennessee?"

"Yes."

The lieutenant never did turn all the way around. He never did ask any return questions of the captain, which would have kept the conversation going in the damp and gloomy morning. The captain shrugged his shoulders and sat back. In his mind, he fixed the lieutenant as one more thing he did not understand in the world, one more thing added to a list that had grown so long since he entered the war. With that list, he did nothing. Once something was placed on the list, the captain ceased to concern himself with it, for he allowed it as something he would not understand if he spent his life trying. The captain thought that the lieutenant might be the first.

Captain Turner had an all-leather duffel bag. During the months of occupation, when he acted as military governor for a small region of Austria, he met an Austrian tailor. The tailor, a small and balding man, told the captain that he would be happy to do any work the captain might ask of him. Never before had the captain had the services of a tailor available to him, and he could think of nothing for weeks, try as he did, for the tailor to do. Finally, he conceived the idea of converting his duffel from canvas to leather. The tailor did the job expertly. He did not ask to be paid for his work. He acted as if it was a privilege to serve the military governor.

Captain Turner paid the man anyway, perhaps more than was necessary, but then he found the money returned under his door the next day.

In his leather duffel, Captain Turner had a bottle of cognac. *That was one thing he would miss at home,* he thought—good liquor for the taking. Also, he had with him two small glasses made of thick French glass. That he would never understand the lieutenant would not prevent him from offering the lieutenant a shot of cognac in thick French glass.

The next day the captain nudged the lieutenant's shoulder with a half-full glass of cognac. "Here, lieutenant, here's a drink to the war's end."

The lieutenant turned just far enough to glance at the offering. Then he turned back and replied, almost too quiet to hear, "No, thank you, Captain. I don't drink."

Captain Turner was not insulted. As he drank down the refused cognac, it was clear that the lieutenant was not being rude or even unfriendly. It seemed to be a matter of preoccupation that was controlling the lieutenant. Captain Turner felt he could do nothing if good cognac could not begin to dislodge him. For the second time, the captain gave up on the lieutenant as they drove on, in silence, except for the wind and the jeep's motor, to Marseilles.

The troop ship, a floating city, was aglow. It was loaded with about five thousand soldiers, of whom roughly one-fifth were commissioned officers. Aboard was a festive, almost brawling atmosphere, as in a boomtown where all the seekers had struck gold. Captain Turner presented his orders to an officer and was assigned quarters in the officer's section of the ship. It was after two a.m., and the ship, unlike the other times the captain had been aboard a transport, was brightly lit.

Throughout the ship were countless games of cards and dice in progress. French radio was broadcast over the public address system.

Though exhausted and badly in need of sleep, the captain deposited his gear and returned to the deck to watch the coast of France give way to the sea. Some citizens of Marseilles had taken to seeing the American ships off. And even at night, at its darkest in the cold and wet, a few were on the docks with their scarves and berets, waving. Captain Turner recalled the steel-like tension, the darkness and quiet, and the cold of the night he landed at. He recalled the breath of death that had been in the air that night and so many nights thereafter, and again he thanked God that it was over. The captain stood without waving back to the French citizens. He was proud that he was a member of an army of liberation rather than one of conquest and domination and oppression. He was thankful, thankful because he believed that the side a soldier lined up on was mostly an accident of birth.

Captain Turner's thoughts were interrupted when he became aware of someone standing near to him in a shadow of the ship's structure. It was Lieutenant Myers.

"Hello, lieutenant," said the captain, smoking.

"Good evening, captain." The lieutenant's voice seemed to come slowly out of the darkness that surrounded him. Perhaps he had been standing there for some time in silence.

"I was watching France. Remembering when we landed."

"I missed the landings by two weeks."

'It was something to miss. When did you get your commission, lieutenant?"

"Early in 1944."

"Were you commissioned out of college?"

"Yes. But not so with you, was it, Captain?'

"No. I was plucked from obscurity. I came in as a private with my local National Guard unit. At some point, they decided to test me. That was the last I saw of the hometown contingent.

"Probably just as well," said the lieutenant. "What?"

"Excuse me, Captain. I say it might have been just as well that you started with the ranks, don't you think?"

The captain nodded. "It didn't hurt, I suppose." He laughed. "There's a risk that way, though. One could easily get lost in the shuffle. How would I have made it through the war without the privilege of rank?"

Lieutenant Myers did not smile or turn toward the captain. He stared at Marseilles. "Or without its' responsibilities?" he asked.

"That too, I guess," said the captain. In silence the captain lit another cigarette and offered one to Lieutenant Myers. By watching the lights of the city, the two could see that they were beginning to sail. Captain Turner dropped the match into the sea, but the flame expired long before it hit the water.

"They say you've been promoted to captain," said Turner.

"I've heard that too," said the lieutenant.

"You don't believe it?"

"I don't believe it or disbelieve it. When something happens, I will believe it."

The captain laughed and nodded his head. "You know, when we came here I didn't know what to believe about anything. Like a child, you had to learn everything over. All you could do was hope to stay alive until you'd learned it for yourself."

"But you did learn, didn't you? And now you have two ways to believe?"

"You can only use one at a time. You had to follow one. You had to believe one or the other."

"That's right," said Lieutenant Myers.

"There was one thing that I always believed," answered Turner. "I always believed that we would win this war."

"I confess, I didn't know that until recently."

"You didn't feel it in your gut from the beginning?"

"Not in any sense."

"No, I didn't even know the time most of the time."

"Well, lieutenant, when you get home you can act as if you were confident of victory from the first day. That is a soldier's prerogative."

"A soldier has a lot of prerogatives, Captain, but pretending is not one of them. My brain would not accept them. My brain told me to work harder, sleep less, and pray more."

The captain laughed lightly and shrugged. "Well, those thoughts got you through the war. Maybe your brain has changed now. Maybe your brain will know when to speak and when to stay quiet."

"Unlikely, Captain, I know my brain."

The captain considered what the lieutenant said and decided that it might be so. He saw that the lights of Marseilles had quickly dimmed in a fog that cut between the ship and the city. The ship was underway to the east, and it would be at least two weeks, if not more; two weeks the captain intended to spend with sleep, cognac, and cards." Maybe you're right, lieutenant. It's over now, though, and I'm glad of it. I need some sleep, but first I need a drink. Will you join me?"

"No, thank you, Captain. I don't drink," said the lieutenant, who remained standing on the deck, peering into the darkness of the night, the sea, and the fog.

Captain Turner woke late the next day. After a meal, he went onto the deck to watch the east float away and the west come his way. The sun was shining, though clouds ringed the horizon. No land could be seen, only blue sea. The air smelled salty.

The captain came to find a group of enlisted men and non- commissioned officers playing craps. A brown army blanket spread on the ship's gray steel plating served as their felt. A dozen men were participants in the game; perhaps two dozen stood witness. Some of the men had their shirts off despite the bright sun. The sea air was chill and misty. Nearly every man had a bottle of some type of liquor, and those bottles were freely shared.

"Have a shot of this fine brandy, captain," called one of the shirtless men, a man half again as old as Captain Turner. The man was pointing his bottle toward the captain. To even the captain's surprise, he accepted the bottle. "Thank you. I will." He did not call the soldier by rank. He knew the man was a private even though the man was out of uniform, but he did not want the man to know that he could read rank on the man's face. "It's good brandy. You were not joking. Thank you."

“Hell no, captain, I don’t joke about brandy,” grinned the private. “I wouldn’t offer a fellow American soldier anything less than the best.”

“It’s damn good,” said the captain. He drank again as he watched the game. The shirtless private rolled the dice, made his number, and collected several dollars. He called to the captain. “Stay around, captain. You bring me luck.”

“What’s the bet?” asked the captain, curious. “Minimum four bits, no maximum.”

The maximum is twelve bits for these dandies,” said a corporal who appeared to be winning. “I’m glad they didn’t fight the war so timidly.”

“This is money, not war,” replied a small man, a private first-class who was not playing.

Captain Turner returned the bottle. “Thank you, soldier. Tell me, where’s the officer’s game?”

“I heard one is being held in Colonel Sorenson’s quarters.”

“At Colonel Sorenson’s quarters?” How did that happen?”

A few of the soldiers around the blanket laughed. One dared to speak up. “Sorenson would have given his quarters over to the enemy if they asked; he’s been promoted by time, not ability.”

“Oh,” said the captain, under his breath.

Captain Turner found a card game in progress at the Sorenson’s former quarters. There was an abundance of liquor in the room. Eight officers, the gamut of rank, were involved in the game. Other officers, not playing, were drinking and watching. The minimum bet was five dollars.

The captain had a good day at the table. He sat down with one hundred fifty dollars, prepared to win what he could or to lose it all, and came away with eight hundred. The game stopped at dusk and was scheduled to start up again in the evening. After the evening meal, after dark, the captain walked to the open deck to smoke. Near the same spot as the night before was Lieutenant Myers, looking like he hadn’t moved or slept. “Hello again, lieutenant.”

“Good evening, captain,”

“I didn’t see you today. There are some good games going. Have you gotten in on any of them?

“No, I haven’t. Have you?”

“Yes. I had a good day. But that’s only today. I’ll be it all again tomorrow. I’ve got nothing to lose now.”

“I suppose that’s one way to look at it.”

"An amateur's way, no doubt." Shrugged the captain.

Both men smoked. The lieutenant asked, "Are you married, Captain?"

"Yes, I have a son."

"Will they meet the ship?"

"If my letter beats me back. And you?"

"My wife… and perhaps my mother?"

"What are you going back to, lieutenant?" The captain looked for the lieutenant's face but could not see it well in the dark. The lieutenant spoke after a minute.

"I don't know; I really do not know."

"Well, what did you leave?"

Lieutenant Myers laughed to himself. "I left a bored man from a boring place."

Captain Turner smiled. "Then I suppose you found the war a great change. I suppose you found out a lot about the world and about yourself."

"You could say that. You could say a lot."

"Considering your rank, you made quite a name for yourself. I heard of you often."

"Yes, but I don't pay any attention."

"That's fine, but you know it independent of what you were told. You could stay with the army."

"No, the army is not for me without a war to fight."

The captain nodded. He drank cognac from a silver flask that he'd found in Berlin. He did not bother to offer any of the liquor to the lieutenant, remembering his abstinence.

"Is that a good cognac you're drinking, Captain?"

"The best."

"Will you be able to get it in the states?"

"Only if I'm rich. In other words, no. This bottle will probably be the end of it."

"If I had some, I'd give it to you, captain."

"You had a reputation for having a stock of quality liquors and wines. I'm surprised to learn that you don't drink."

"I used liquor as gifts. Sometimes I gave bottles away in order to receive favors and sometimes as nothing more than gifts for good work."

"Were you looking for liquor in Lindau?"

"Yes. You know about Lindau?"

"That's when I first heard your name."

The lieutenant took a deep breath before answering. "I'm not surprised. It's the worst part of the war for me. You can imagine that I have no interest in reliving it." The captain took a deep breath before saying, "Understood, but the soldiers who were with you spread it like wildfire, but you know how that goes."

Lieutenant Myers nodded. "It was a terrible decision I had to make, Captain, but with the position I'm in, I better get used to talking about it as much as I hate doing it. I might as well start with you… Lindau is a small village in southern Germany. I came to it with my artillery-scouting unit. We were on a small hill overlooking the town when we met up with another unit that was commanded by Captain Cox. The town seemed abandoned, and I was interested in whether the town was occupied and, of course, a little bit of liquor for a cold night."

"And your other soldiers were interested in a few things also?" said Captain Turner.

"That's right. The problem was that Captain Cox maintained that the town was deserted and he was ready to go down. I had a feeling that it was not empty, but there was nothing to prove it to Captain Cox. I wanted to call in a few rounds of artillery before we went in. Captain Cox laughed at me. He said he couldn't wait that long and that artillery would destroy the goods he wanted. As a superior officer, he ordered us to go down into the town."

"I never heard that part," said Captain Turner.

"No, of course not. I never told that part before. Anyhow, I refused.

My refusal was not taken seriously by Captain Cox. He laughed again. He figured my discipline for refusal would come when I was denied a share in the booty."

"A serious error in judgment by Captain Cox."

"As it turned out. Five of my men stayed behind with me. They survived. Fourteen accompanied Captain Cox. Their only arms were their rifles and a machine gun mounted jeep in which Captain Cox rode. When they reached the shop where the liquor was, they all went inside, leaving no guard. We were watching when a unit of about twenty Germans came out from an adjacent building. They walked right up behind our boys. We fired our gun and yelled, but we were too far off to be of any help. We heard machine gun fire from the

German troops behind our boys. They had simply walked up, and they did not lose a boy or a man. Then they came into the street cheering. When artillery caught up with us, we pounded the town to ash, but it didn't do any good. Nothing did any good."

After a minute, Captain Turner spoke, "You were a hero for the five that followed your intuition, Lieutenant Myers."

Lieutenant Myers was choked up and had tears. "But we lost fourteen simply because I was unable to convince Captain Cox. Fourteen I will never forget. Fourteen whose doors I will knock on back home."

Again, the lieutenant remained in place when the captain took his leave. The night was clear and cold. Captain Turner did not dwell long on what thoughts kept the lieutenant standing alone on the deck; they did not need dwelling; they were obvious. He did wonder, however, if the lieutenant was getting any sleep, for he had the appearance of a man several days into combat. Yet, his conversation had been existent for the first time, and he was quite alert, so the captain thought no more about it. Captain Turner won again on his second day of play; he more than doubled his money. The losses were spread among many men, all good officers, and there were no hard feelings. After a meal and a second hot shower for the day, Captain Turner returned to the open deck, curious as to whether the lieutenant might still be at his self -assigned post. He was. "Are you getting any sleep, Lieutenant?" asked the captain.

"Some—in the day. Why? Do I look ragged?"

"A little. Why not at night?"

"Can't."

"Any specific reason?"

"Must be a reason." The lieutenant did not offer more. Fatigue was in his eyes and his voice. He wore his heavy wool overcoat against the cold sea air. He hadn't shaved for days, at least since boarding the ship.

"Did you win today, captain?" he asked.

"Yes, I was a winner tonight."

"Good. Do you gamble at home? Are you a gambler?"

"No. Some, but never compared to this."

"Is it in your blood now—after winning so much?"

"I don't think so. I won't gamble after we reach the States."

"That's wise. Listen, captain." The lieutenant frowned. "Is it alright for me to be talking to you like this? You do outrank me."

"Forget about that rank stuff. There's no need for it anymore. We are headed for home, where this rank means nothing."

The lieutenant nodded. "You're right, I guess. I appreciate it. What do you plan to do with your winnings—if you have made plans already?"

"I'll have to wait until I get off the ship to see if I have any money left.

I'm getting more reckless each day I gamble. I guess land will force me to decide. This ship is like floating in the sky. Nothing is real, nothing is clear."

"Do you have work waiting for you, Captain?"

"At my father's hardware store, if nothing else. And you?"

"No, nothing waiting. I haven't given it any thought. But it's not so important for me. I haven't a son."

"My wife writes that my son is a curious rat."

The lieutenant smiled at the captain and asked with a little devilishness, "Did you leave any children in Europe?"

After a minute of silence, the captain answered, "It's possible, I suppose. I know I left behind some cheap jewelry, some liquor, and war goods to keep a person warm."

The lieutenant smiled again. "Me too, I guess. And this will be the last time I will speak of it."

The next day was the captain's best day at gambling. He did not seem to be able to lose an important hand. Other officers continued to play against him because they were certain that no man's luck could endure as long as the captain's did that day. They felt that if they stayed with him, he would begin to lose, and when the bottom fell out, it would fall all the way, and they would be in a position to recoup their losses. Other officers, those who gambled very little, came around to the game upon hearing of Captain Turner's phenomenal streak of gambler's fortune. Even those good men, convinced upon watching the captain's excessive and reckless betting, laid down bets. They felt that they had come at just the right time, just after the captain's luck had peaked but when he was still betting as wildly and heavily as winners do. But they were wrong that day.

Captain Turner's luck did not change. In any case, his winnings had reached nine thousand. In paper and promise, the captain had another two thousand, but this money he had allowed in only because he felt so good. He did not want to say no to anything for fear that it would break the streak. Twice during the long day, the captain saw Lieutenant Myers pass by the gambling room. The lieutenant did not stop, and he did not bother to look into the room as he passed. The lieutenant's clothes were the same wrinkled ones he'd had on the night before. When the game broke for dinner, the captain ate and then searched for Lieutenant Myers on the open-air deck.

"I've earned a farm by gambling, lieutenant." Laughed the captain, finding the lieutenant where he had expected.

"Well, congratulations, captain. What will you do with your farm?" "Farm it unless I lose it before this ship docks."

"Oh, so you have enough money to buy a farm?"

"Only enough for a good down payment."

"You should quit, Captain."

"I can't quit yet. We've got two more days at sea.

"You might lose the farm if you don't quit," said the lieutenant. Captain Turner smiled. "It won't matter either way. If I do, I'll work some job for a few years until I have the money again."

The lieutenant shook his head. I don't believe you could lose the farm. You're too much of a farmer."

Captain Turner chuckled and responded, "Actually, I can't see myself other than as a soldier."

The lieutenant nodded, smiling. "We can hope," he said with a wry smile. Both men lit cigarettes and smoked in silence, into the dark. They leaned over the rail to watch the fluorescent foam spilled aside by the ship's keel. The captain went to his quarters and returned with cognac and a plan for the future. "I have to get in on all of the celebrating I can," he said. "Right now there's nothing to do but thank the many gods for life and victory. Soon everything will be back with some version of normality."

The lieutenant looked over to the captain and smiled. He did not seem to be listening but was waiting. When the captain stopped talking, the lieutenant spoke. There was an extreme weariness in his eyes and voice; in his voice, a wheeze.

"Captain, did you know a Lieutenant Colonel Nelson?"

"No, I don't think so. What army?"

"The third."

"I don't recall the name."

"He's dead now."

"During the war?"

"He was superior to my regiment."

"Was he helpful to your regiment?"

"No."

The captain indicated that he understood. "And it seems there is no way to get rid of them if you're under them. They seem to sense that you question their orders, and then they lay even more on you."

The lieutenant did not hesitate to describe his view of Lieutenant Colonel Nelson. "He was responsible for at least fifty allied deaths through simple incompetence. Surely there were many more that I knew nothing about or which occurred before me."

"A career?"

"Yes."

"It's a shame when that happens," said the captain, shaking his head." "It's intolerable in combat!" The lieutenant's voice betrayed more emotion than the captain had heard him use before, but it had escaped like a hissing leak, one that the lieutenant quickly patched.

"What became of him? Do you know?"

"He came once to our battery position when we were firing support for the infantry."

"Did you know then of his incompetence?"

"Yes. All artillerymen knew his reputation. He always rode my back. Our opinions were ignored. We could not trust him or his decisions."

"I can see that. It's a terrible position to be in."

"One day he came; we were on a hill, firing over the next hill. There were four guns firing. I was calling range and fire orders. There was a ravine between the two hills."

"Where was the infantry?"

"Six-thousand meters ahead of us."

"And the enemy?"

"Roughly nine-thousand meters. I had spotters set up on the rise of the second hill. They could see everything."

"What did this Lieutenant Colonel Nelson do?"

"He came up in a jeep and asked the range. I told him I was sending fire all around nine thousand meters. He became enraged and said we were having no effect. He told me the enemy was at six-thousand and that I had the wrong info."

“Six-thousand! What had he seen, his own infantry?”

“God doesn’t know; I don’t know. He wouldn’t listen to me, and he wouldn’t answer questions I asked. He ordered our range to drop to six-thousand meters. That I could not do. That’s where OUR soldiers were.”

“Nelson must have been far away to make those mistakes.”

“Oh sweet Jesus, you couldn’t follow that order.”

“No, I told myself that I would never repeat what happened with Lieutenant Cox. Lieutenant Nelson drove away in his jeep, down the hill, into the ravine that was about twelve thousand meters distant. I was paralyzed with frustration and anger. Then our intelligence notified us that the Germans were entering the ravine and had the jump on us.”

Captain Turner paused, unable to speak. Eventually he said, “I’ve never heard of a soldier in that position…” And before he could speak any more, the lieutenant spoke clearly and strongly, “The number one gun was loaded. The gunner asked the range. I answered, Twelve-thousand meters. The second gunner loaded and requested range. Twelve thousand meters. The third gunner was watching me as I watched him. “Twelve-thousand fifty meters, I called. The fourth was called in at twelve thousand meters. I dropped my concern of where Lieutenant Colonel was except for our radio man to send code that fire was being sent at twelve-thousand and for all to abandon all areas in that area; artillery was working.”

Captain Turner fell into disbelief and silence. The lieutenant continued, “The gunners stood at their artillery, ready. They stared at me. All of them did, silently waiting. I ordered fire. And they fired. I did not hesitate.”

After a minute, the captain was still staring directly at the lieutenant.

When he spoke, he said, “Why are you telling this to me now?” he asked. “Because it’s true. Because I have to tell someone, so I can’t deny it later when it comes out. I had two choices. I wasn’t going to follow the wrong choice ever again. I wasn’t going to kill or maim my brothers.”

“But why tell me?”

“Because you have rank and experience, and because I had to tell somebody, and because you understand war situations, I’m not entirely sure I’d mind if you told the world.”

The captain shook his head, leaning slightly over the railing toward the sea. “Can you live with this, lieutenant?”

"Captain, I admire you more than anyone I've ever encountered, and you're probably the only person I could have told this to, but I would say that the question might be, 'Could I live with a hundred dead American soldiers?'"

"I accept that, Lieutenant, and I recognize that war has no answer, and I pray for you and your memory. War demands untold decisions. I promise you that I and no one else is entitled to judge you. What I can urge you to do is to forget it if you want to live in peace."

"You're right, captain, but I doubt that I will."

Captain Turner did not sleep that night. He could not stop thinking of the young lieutenant and what he experienced. The captain wanted an end to war stories. He wanted to see his wife, his son, and his home. He wanted an end to foreign names and places. He sat up in bed with a light for a good part of the night, drinking from his last bottle. At one point, the captain dressed and walked in the cold of midnight to where the lieutenant stood, and still the lieutenant was there, facing the sea. The captain could think of nothing more to say to the lieutenant and decided not to approach him. Walking back to his quarters, the captain heard the celebration of small groups of soldiers who were drinking, gambling, and returning home.

The captain listened to the men for a while and then returned to his quarters. He did not sleep the rest of the night, and when he woke in the morning, he was still dressed, and the bottle of liquor was on the table, open and half-empty.

Captain Turner felt rough. He did not shave or shower and did not feel like eating. Now there was not much more than a day before the ship was due to reach the States. The anticipation was no longer dreamlike. It was real and within sight, and Captain Turner wanted to wait no longer. He wanted to run instead of walk the remaining distance; to push the clocks and reach home ground in one quick jump so that nothing more could happen. A massive and lengthy effort was one day shy of being complete, and the captain feared the last day.

The captain played cards on the last day at sea. He played, mainly, as a way to pass time. He felt anxious, and his card playing reflected the way he felt. Just as the day before he was unable to lose, this day he was unable to win. First, he lost the paper promises, and then the losses stared to eat his cash. The captain did not care about losing. He only hoped that the nine thousand would be sufficient to keep him in the game for the whole of the last day. If losing it all was enough to get him through the last day, it would be worth it to him. The other players were gay and laughed about the captain's sudden and great change of fortune. Captain Turner did not mind their jokes, just as he did not mind losing.

At dusk, the captain was down to three thousand. A second lieutenant came through the gambling quarters and informed all present that the ship's anticipated arrival at Virginia was eleven a.m. the following day. The players decided to take their meals where they sat in order to continue the game, a decision that was approved by the captain. A crowd of enlisted men as well as officers had gathered around the players as the game had boiled down to the big money game of the ship. Captain Turner sent a private to his quarters to fetch his half-bottle. For a time after the meal, the captain's luck turned good, and he began to bet heavily, which excited the crowd. It seemed that the entire ship was in and about the gambling quarters, and most were pulling for the captain. When he started losing again, he did not stop the heavy betting. He was drinking the remainder of his bottle. He figured that he could coincide the last of the cognac with the end of his money and the onset of an exhaustion that would permit him to sleep the last night through.

After midnight, the captain had only five hundred dollars of gambling money and a few swallows of cognac left. The ship's siren began to wail. The gamblers and their spectators believed the siren to be related to land sighting, and they cheered. But then a soldier pushed his way into the room yelling, "Man overboard, man overboard!"

The captain's throat went dry. He rose, without hurrying, and followed the crowd scrambling to the ship's port side. There were spotlights on the cold, dark water with the sirens that continued their cry, but nothing could be seen. A lifeboat manned by three sailors was being lowered into the water. All the soldiers on the ship were at the rail, searching with their eyes.

Captain Turner stepped back from the crowd. He climbed to the top deck. The lieutenant was not in his place. Where the lieutenant had been, now three of the ship's commanding officers were in his place.

"We will never find him, but we have to try," said one of the officers, peering over the side. "We never leave a soldier behind, but we will never find him."

"He wouldn't have jumped," said another.

"There's no reason for it."

"Now of all times a soldier wouldn't jump. Certainly he fell. Too much drink, probably. But don't put that in the report. Otherwise his family might be denied his money."

"Of course it was an accident," confirmed the third officer. "And I agree with you—it was no doubt liquor that tripped him up."

"Good," said the third officer. "We should be underway after the search has been conducted. Maybe another forty minutes."

"Fine, sir."

Captain Turner sighed and spoke to himself: "*It was a Soldier's Prerogative.*" In Search of a Dry Place to Sleep.

Part One:
In Search of a Mexican Bar

I count Roberto Ortiz as a friend. At least it is my belief that we are good, trustworthy friends. I don't know much about his family, his past, his problems, or his desires for the future. It is true that I really do not know much about the inside of him, like his secrets, but I haven't made any special efforts to do so. I don't know how Roberto views our friendship, if he sees it as I do or not, for I have never discussed it with him. Maybe he sees it differently. It doesn't matter very much at our age as long as we agree that we are friends and that we can rely on each other.

Roberto and I are graduate students together. Like all of us, he is somewhat poor, but poor doesn't really matter at our age. In fact, it is safe to say that we believe that the stoic endurance of poverty and the ultimate rising up from its' grasp are good for one's character. Most of us understand that poverty has many meanings. For sure, 'poverty' to one person is comfort to another. Being from Mexico, Roberto might look at poverty from a different lens, and I would certainly respect that.

On the first day of spring break, Roberto found me in a bar near the university drinking beer. His way of greeting me was to call out loud, "Hey, let's go to Mexico for a few days." His Spanish accent was strong but easy to follow. His hair was black and shiny, and his skin was a smooth brown.

He had neither a beard nor a mustache. He wore worker's boots, denims, and a serape. He was pushing six feet in height.

"Sure," I said. Going to Mexico was not difficult, living so near the border and sharing the Sonoran Desert. "Where shall we go?"

"My hometown, Cananea."

"Perfecto. Let's see if Margo wants to go."

"Good idea; she's usually up for something crazy."

Roberto Ortiz was not born in the United States. He came with his mother at fifteen years old to live in Arizona, and he had papers that allowed him to be in the United States. He learned English by running with the Anglo boys in the public schools. He spent a few years in the army after high school, stationed in Panama and also at the army's special languages school in Monterey. I'd always suspected that the army failed to convince him to stay in the army as some kind of spy. By the time I met Roberto, he was thoroughly political and very much the antithesis of an American patriot, but he had no intention of moving back to Mexico—he was naturalized as a citizen. I attended the ceremony. The United States Attorney, a short man with a skin disease, dressed in a three-piece suit, presented the group to the federal judge for the official swearing of loyalty to the United States. The Daughters of the American Revolution gave out little 3' by 5" inch plastic flags and donuts. Roberto disposed of the little flag discreetly and took two donuts. He was the first one out the door.

Our friend Margo was twenty-five, our school classmate. Like Roberto, Margo was a naturalized citizen. Her birth country was Germany, and her accent left no doubt of it even though her English was quite clear. Despite the fact that spring break had started, we found her in the library, as we knew we would. We greeted her by saying, "We're going to Mexico for a few days. Come with us!"

Margo took a deep breath, exhaled, and said, "I shouldn't, but you know what? I can't resist an invitation to Mexico. I've never been. You two will be great guides. Sure, I'll go."

Margo had a blonde roommate of great beauty but of little intelligence. This woman, Sylvia, tantalized Roberto even in his dreams. "Do you think Sylvia would like to come?" I asked Margo. "I hoped she would say no."

"No," said Margo. "Her fiancé is coming soon to visit her."

"Sylvia is getting married?" I was dumbfounded. It was easy to see why a man who had only seen Sylvia would be willing to die for a night of her love, but any man who had ever conversed with her would have to be nuts to commit a perfectly good life to her. "Who is it?" I asked.

"No one you know; a fellow who beats her and yells obscenities at her. She enjoys speaking in obscenities."

"Sylvia?"

Margo merely rolled her eyes and shrugged her shoulders. When we were in the car, Margo's car, and headed south, Roberto spoke: "I want that woman," he said, "as a statement of challenge rather than passion."

"You want her for one night," I said.

"That's what I mean," said Roberto, as if his statement was incapable of being misunderstood. Margo laughed. I was driving. Roberto was in the back seat.

"I really want that woman," he said again after a time of silence to make sure we knew the depth of his desire, driving through the desert.

I don't know why, but I felt the devious pleasure that sometimes wells up in me when I know something another person doesn't and which, when told, would crush some dream or desire. Apparently, Margo had the same thought. She glanced at me with a grin to see which of us would say it. "Too late," I said, looking to Roberto through the mirror. "She's going to be wed really soon to a wife beater and pornographer." Margo laughed. "Not a pornographer. A man who enjoys being obscene."

"Same thing," I said. "Besides, what would you have talked about once you were in bed with her?"

"I wouldn't be talking, amigo. But you probably wouldn't know." "Sometime you have to talk to her, amigo."

"Not in bed, mi amigo."

"But sooner or later."

"Bueno. Later, then. Afterward."

"Alright. Not until afterwards. But you still have to talk to the woman."

"By then it doesn't matter, does it?"

Margo snorted and shook her head. Margo did not usually bother arguing with either Roberto or me. She laughed and shrugged us off as harmless males except for our most drastic violations of the rights of women. She knew when we were intentionally talking shit to get under her skin.

Like Roberto, Margo was not born in the United States. Her motherland was Germany. She had married a U.S. serviceman when she was sixteen and came to America when she was seventeen. She proceeded with the task of learning English by reading English literature and watching cartoons on television. I have suspected that every phase of Margo's life had been manipulated to get her to America—probably by her mother, who had surely suffered desperately during World War II. Margo had a son by the serviceman, moved with him to America, and not long after gaining legal status in the United States, divorced the young man.

I cannot remember ever seeing a border patrol agent of any nationality who was not fat. At the Mexican border, the officers were distinguished from the

American officers by their mustaches. Their mustache might be as wide and thick as a good paintbrush or as thin as a pencil line, but all of them are from the north of Mexico, and therefore they have a mustache.

A fat border man with a desk job and a mustache stepped to the counter. He spoke only Spanish and never did look at me. As is common with political types, Roberto had a passport and dual citizenship, so he did not need a visa. I heard him giving Margo's information to the agent, and after passing a few dollars to the agent, he had Margo's visa. In Spanish, he told the agent that I was Margo's husband, and he told me to pass a few dollars to the agent, and again, in no time, I had my visa with a new last name. Leaving the office, Roberto was laughing deeply. "I got you across the border, and I got you married. I can't wait to tell Margo that you and she are now married and that she has to sleep with you tonight."

"Never happen," I said, not sure whether I should be angry or amused. Only time would tell, I figured.

Inside of Mexico, we stopped for gasoline at a so-called service station. Roberto and I headed for the toilet, where we both gagged at the toilet and the stench. We held our breath. It was nothing short of foul.

The door was jammed and would not close. The toilet was clogged, and the washbowl was cracked apart. Roberto reached for the light, which did not work. "Typical," he said, with disgusted emotion.

At a liquor store, we bought a quart of tequila and a small sack of bright green limes. We drove on the road that led to Hermosillo, paralleling the railroad tracks. Roberto drove now. Margo was in the back seat. The Mexicans still mark the sites of fatal accidents along the highway with small white crosses, names and dates, and red, green, and blue plastic flowers. Along the highway, frequent religious scenes are housed in the stone hives, often with candles burning, cared for by a silent guardian.

We drove south for a short distance and then turned back on a road heading northeast, toward the first east-west mountains inside Mexico. In the middle of those mountains, within shouting distance of the U.S. border, was the town of Cananea. Cananea was Roberto's town of birth. It was a copper mining town. Regarding copper towns, there is one certain fact: copper is the unilateral and controlling force; the mine is by far the dominant factor that controls everything. The mine is the reason for the town. Copper mines have been known to swallow up the town that surrounds it in the ravenous pursuit of the mother lode, a la Butte.

Montana. Even so, even so, if the copper disappeared one day, so too would the company and their machinery and the people and their belongings and their animals. In the end, the very end, the shaft and the earth as well.

Cananea had copper, but even more significant, it had the great distinction that the Mexican Revolution started in that small mountain town so far to the north. In the years of opposition against the very long-standing dictatorship of Porfirio Diaz, there often occurred labor strikes as a favored source of agitation and political education for the workers and the peasants.

One such strike, be it pure or revolutionary-inspired, occurred at the Cananea copper mine in 1906. Slaughter was the answer to labor unrest. But the slaughterers were not Mexicans, no, for the Cananea copper mine was owned by the Americans, so it was Americans who pulled the triggers to protect American interests with the acquiescence and approval of Mexican authorities—sufficient reason for any good citizen to join or start a revolution, I suppose.

The road to Cananea is narrow, two narrow lanes. The upside of the road smears the mountain, and the downside is a canyon to be avoided at any cost, including a head-on collision. Roberto insisted on driving this section, and he drove it as if he had built the road and as if he owned it. He drove, and he talked. The only vegetation was agave and yucca plants. I thought what an eyesore our crumpled car would be at the bottom of the canyon.

There was rain and wind when we arrived in the town. It was late afternoon, though not dark. Cananea is an old town, built in a bowl, roughly surrounded and protected by the mountains. The center of town is the lowest spot, and the streets go up in either direction, quite steeply. Most of the homes are clapboard painted with wild and striking colors. The commercial buildings are built of stone and adobe. In the center of town is a large plaza, the zocalo, which is three blocks long, one block wide, grassy, and filled with mature trees. There are park benches and a gazebo in the center of the plaza.

"Let's eat," said Roberto. He started walking up the steep sidewalk toward a cantina that looked quite able to provide both food and drink.

Men and boys came down the sidewalk, squeezing by Margo in a way that ensured that they would make contact with her as they passed. There was no inhibition in their stares; they made love to her with their eyes. They looked at Roberto and me with a grin and a wink, a universal language between men.

It wasn't until we sat down to eat that I noticed a change had come over Roberto. It wasn't a great change, but his spirits seemed to be dampened. I saw that Margo had also noticed; she reacted differently to him, more cautiously, as if she did not understand his behavior, as if the status quo had been upset by some unknown cause. I had seen this before and wondered if it might be a result of communicating in a language that was native to neither of them.

We ate a plate of tacos with Mexican beer to wash them down. The taco shells were still warm and greasy from being fried up as little corn tortillas in a shell. They weren't uniform in size or even pre-shaped as they are in the U.S. The salsa was not hot, but it was spicy and good. Roberto and I were the only men in the place. The rest of the patrons were women and children. One door at the back of the room led to the kitchen, but there was another door. Roberto saw me looking.

"There's a bar on the other side," he offered almost as a challenge."

"Is it normal for men and women to separate where you eat and drink?" asked Margo.

Roberto smiled knowingly as if we were his clueless children. He answered, "Of course. No one would have it any other way. That's how they like it."

I looked around the little cafe, remembering that I'd seen no other men. Roberto was watching Margo. I said, "Is our dignity impaired by being in here with the women and children instead of in the bar?" I asked. Roberto shrugged, adding more salsa to his food. "No, I think not."

"These people are used to it. North Americans come in here with their women. Mexicans let their women come in alone. They wait for the women in the bar. When the woman is finished and ready to go, she sends a messenger, usually a son, into the bar to get the man. Sometimes she must wait. There is no way the man will hurry a beer to answer a woman's summons."

"Oh Christ!" said Margo, clearly offended.

"So if we were Mexican, it would not be dignified to be in here; is that how it is?"

"I am Mexican," said Roberto.

"I'm aware of that. I mean, if we were Mexican living in this town where everyone knew us."

"One's dignity does not depend on where he lives or who he knows," said Roberto with a smile. "A man carries his dignity with him before even his traveling bag."

Deciding to get more deeply involved, I said, "That might be true, but it would be worse to have a loss of dignity at home where your family and friends are." Roberto was nodding as a patient instructor nods. "You're right. I don't feel I've suffered a serious loss of dignity." He winked at Margo.

"This dignity thing is a fragile entity, isn't it?" said Margo. "Fragile and precious," answered Roberto.

"Primitive," said Margo.

"As primitive as Hitler," responded Roberto quickly with a touch of sharpness.

Margo stared at Roberto for a minute, apparently unable to believe what she heard. "No, not that primitive," she said finally, adding, "but that wasn't necessary."

Roberto shrugged. "Perhaps it wasn't," he said, "but I'm sick of insults to Mexico when she is surrounded by bestiality and neurosis."

"Call me neurotic," I said.

"I will," said Roberto, "whenever it's necessary."

"Call me Margo," said Margo. "Let's get a beer next door." I took a step back to avoid any incoming, but none came.

"I've done half of it," said Roberto with resignation. "I might as well do it all." With those words, he opened the door that led from the cafe to the bar. Margo followed without hesitation. I brought up the silent rear.

The bar was a corner building. Two walls looked onto the street. The floor was Saltillo tile. Most of the light filtering into the room came from store lights outside and across the street. There was still rain and wind in the night, but it had grown no worse.

At the bar, five or six men were sitting and half as many standing.

There were wood tables, some occupied, around the floor space. The bar fell silent. Every patron watched us as we entered, and, of course, they focused on Margo, examining her from head to toe with a grin that spoke without words.

Margo pretended not to notice their eyes. While she didn't behave as if she had liberated the Cananea Bar, she was quite relaxed.

The bartender came to our table with an apron wrapped about his waist. He was a strong, good-looking man with a full mustache. In Spanish, Roberto ordered three beers while the bartender took the opportunity to get a good look at Margo, and she, to his surprise, took the same opportunity with him.

By the second beer, the novelty of Margo had somewhat worn off.

The local men kept the jukebox playing, and when Roberto took his turn at music selection, the Mexicans were quite pleased with his choice. By his choices, Roberto was able to prove his tribal province. They tipped their beers to him and discussed the harsh rain that kept them indoors.

After cursing myself for the hundredth time for not learning Spanish, I turned to Roberto and said, "Donde esta el bano?" Roberto pointed to a curtain behind and to the side of the bar.

I went to the curtain, pulled it back, and entered. It was only a small opening in the wall about the size of a closet. Against one sidewall were four cardboard boxes stacked in twos. I wondered if I was in the wrong place, a supply closet perhaps. There was no sign, and Roberto was in one of those moods. I'd truly hate to urinate in a supply closet in a foreign country. But against the back wall and at the floor was a narrow trough with a drain in the middle. There was no water running down the wall and no pipes where any water could be released, but there was a bucket of water against the wall opposite the supplies. I was standing with only the thin curtain separating me from the barroom and its patrons. I didn't know what to do. Suddenly the curtain flew back like a swift bird taking flight, but only for a second to allow one of the patrons to enter the "closet." He smiled at me, zipped down his jeans, freed his penis, and peed against the back wall, and then splashed a bit of water from the bucket against the back wall and smiled once again as he departed. Now I understood and utilized what I had learned before silently returning to my chair.

I went to the bar to refurnish our beer when I heard the bartender's deep voice speak to Margo in Spanish, which neither she nor I could understand, but when I heard everyone in the bar laughing, I turned and saw Margo enter the so-called bathroom. Then I heard Roberto laughing. It took him at least thirty seconds to gather himself and to call out to Margo, "There's no women's bathroom in here, Margo: you have to go next door where the women and children are."

“You son-of-a-bitch, Roberto,” said Margo, which everyone in the bar understood whether they could speak English or not. At the same time, the patrons called out to me, I presumed, buenos noches senior, lifting their glasses and calling out once again to me. I opened my arms to all of them and answered, “Salud.” Unfortunately, that was the same time that Margo escaped the latrine. The Mexican men cut loose again, calling out in unison, “Buenas noches, jovencita.” To her credit, Margo was prepared. She waved to the men and tossed her underwear high into the air, where it became hooked in the ceiling fan. There was noise and approval for Margo that would make a bullfighter proud.

But Margo’s sense of humor did not reach our table. With sufficient anger in her voice, she turned to Roberto. “Why didn’t you tell me?”

“You didn’t ask,” answers an unrepentant Roberto. “But you knew I was following Stewart.”

“You didn’t ask,” Roberto repeated. “You should know better than to blindly follow a man around.”

“But you knew what I was doing.”

“It was harmless,” dismissed Roberto with a wave of his hand. “It was,” allowed Margo with a smile. “Funny too.”

Roberto nodded to her and then called to the bartender with a camaraderie that did not previously exist: “Señor, tres mas cervezas por favor.”

Margo poked Roberto while he was speaking with the bartender.

“Tell him for me that I think he has a simply charming place here and that I will bring all my girlfriends here to see it.”

“You will have to learn Spanish if you wish to communicate some message to these people.”

“I don’t care that I can’t understand it,” I said. “I’d like to, but I still think it’s beautiful to hear. It flows so smoothly.”

“That’s probably why they include it as one of the romantic languages,” said Roberto.

“My calling myself beautiful does not make it so,” said Margo. “German is also a wonderful sound to the ear.”

“I don’t think so,” said Roberto while I frowned. “I’d say it is harsh and guttural.”

“It is not,” said Margo, her native pride fired up. “You should hear opera in German.”

"I'd rather skip that," said Roberto. "Listen to this, though." Roberto leaned toward Margo, over his beer, as if he was teaching the language by showing the movement of the tongue. Softly, with exact pronunciation, he spoke: {in Spanish} "The spring of the year is for lovers."

Margo, unlinking, mirrored Roberto and leaned toward him as he had leaned toward her. {In German} "It is starting to rain quite hard outside." Roberto made one gentle shake of his head as if he understood the German and was rejecting it. He leaned both toward Margo and the tabletop. He lowered his voice but raised his hand for use in expression.

{Lovers make love in every green field of this grand country."}

Margo tossed this offering off with a facial expression common to the Italians. She leaned closer yet to the table, lowered her voice, and spoke like she was the wind. {"This is the language of the great artists; writers and musicians; painters don't count.}

With his head, less than a foot from hers and flat on the table, speaking in a whisper I could barely hear, Roberto said: {"But even this language is too crude for me. That I could know the tongue of the Aztecs and Toltecs."}

Margo moved within inches, almost whispering into his face: {"You forget the old language fast. I've given up the old tongue for the language of change."}

And there I was, watching the both of them. They were between the windows and me, and I could see their faces, inches apart, eyeing each other and speaking whispered native tongues foreign to my ears. There was quite a lot of rain now, and the usual harshness of the street's neon lights was muted and dulled as the light passed through the falling rain. It was as if the water was colored red, blue, and green; it looked soft and pleasant, like a dream. Still, I felt a little inadequate as I watched and listened to the Mexican and the German. I've always felt that a person accomplished in a second language had a touch of genius, like having two brains as well as the ability to work equally well in either. These bilingual people had an advantage over the rest of us. They can see things two different ways. They can understand, love, hate, or fight in two ways. They can formulate plans and answers in two ways. But most of all, I thought, they have two perspectives, two processes to put the same material through.

When I spoke, I said, "In plain English, I inform both of you that it is raining very hard now. I further inform you that we have some camping gear but no proper rain gear and no tent, and if the weather keeps up, camping is highly unlikely."

"We will have to get a room," said Margo.

Roberto shook his head. "I'm not renting a room in my hometown. I won't stay in a hotel like a tourist in my own town."

Neither Margo nor I had reason to doubt him, but it left us in a spot. Neither of us was inclined to abandon him, but the rain and wind were starting to look like a serious storm that didn't give a damn about us.

Margo's car was a Volkswagen Bug (of course) and hardly sufficient for three grown people to sleep in. To try to stay out of doors with the gear we had would be nonsense. I started to wonder how long the bars in Mexico stayed open.

"Well, what are we going to do then?" asked Margo. She always wanted to know what was going to happen next. But men often did not know, and they did not want the women to know that they did not know. "We can't stay outside in this," she said, gesturing toward the window but leaving her eyes on Roberto. I remained silent, knowing I could rely on Margo to pursue the cause. Roberto did not answer for a minute, but then a sly grin came across his face. "Let's go see Kathy," he said.

Now Margo broke into a grin. "Perhaps she will suggest that we sleep on her floor or maybe the guest room for the female and the floor for you two."

To my surprise, I had completely forgotten about Kathy. In fact, I knew very little about her. For example, I didn't know if Roberto first knew her in Cananea or if he first knew her at our university in Tucson, but in either event, I did know that they sometimes saw each other. I knew also that Kathy was an American. Her father was the president of the Cananea Copper Mine, but he made sure that his daughters were born in the United States. All her life she had lived in Cananea (with frequent shopping trips to America with her mother). When she reached college age, she was sent to university in Arizona. I had met her once, briefly, and there was absolutely nothing to suggest that she had grown up in Mexico; nothing save the perfect Spanish she spoke.

"I'll call and see if she is home," said Roberto.

While Roberto searched for a public phone, Margo turned to me. "I hope she's there. I don't want to sleep in the mud. I've never slept in the mud. I've never met Kathy before either."

"She's Roberto's Mexican girlfriend, but only in the United States." "Oh, I see. Has Roberto met any of her family?"

"Not that I know of."

"Oh, Christ," said Margo. "This is going to be unique."

"It's likely to be a lot more than that. Buckle up."

Roberto returned. "She's home. She said we could come up."

"Have you ever met Kathy's family before?" I asked him. Roberto smiled and shook his head.

"Well," I began. "It's still better than the mud as long as the roof doesn't leak."

"This roof will not leak," Roberto said to me.

"Does Kathy's family know that you see her at the university?" Roberto shrugged his shoulders. "I know who they are," he said.

"Everyone in this town knows who the boss gringos are. Her father is the mine president. He should treat the workers better; provide safety precautions, and better pay. He doesn't provide any safety precautions. The pay is a form of theft from the workers. He doesn't know who I am. Not yet."

"Is the tequila in the car?" I asked.

"I hope so," said Margo. She looked directly into Roberto's eyes and said, "Do you think we could keep in mind that we are looking for a place to sleep away from this hurricane—instead of trying to start a worker's uprising?"

"Depends on how he treats us punks." Roberto smiled.

"Let's go," he said.

Part Two:
In Search of the American/Mexican Girl

We called good-bye to the bar patrons, even Margo did, and stepped outside. The rain and wind seemed much harder than they had from inside the bar. Around the corner and down half of the block on the town's main street was the car. From where the car was parked, a good deal of the town could be seen. I asked Roberto where the house of his childhood was. He answered by having me follow his vision down the hill to the road's bottom and then along a narrow ravine that cut off to the left of the road. In the ravine was crammed a multitude of box-houses, one leaning against the next, looking more like they were washed down the ravine than planned construction. The box-homes were all colors, like a quilt.

The house of Kathy was a distance out and away from the town. The road soon left the paving and turned to mud. The road was straight and flat and deep with ruts from previous cars; the road had been built solely for the house we were headed toward. There were no other homes along the road, which ended at the mine President's front door. The driveway was a red-bricked half circle upon which we deposited a great deal of mud. In the middle of the driveway was a fountain of water illuminated by eight colored lights, each light coloring a different shot of water, all of which converged in the middle of the fountain. The falling rain impaired the splendor of the fountain.

The house was palatial, nearly surrounding us when we stepped from the car. The rain still came, and it was utterly black in every direction except behind us, where there was a dim glow in the lower sky from the lights of Cananea. Though I couldn't see, I figured that the house was built on a flat spot with a view of the mountains or a canyon behind it. I walked over to the fountain, and Roberto and Margo came up behind me.

"Big place the mine President has," I said.

"It is," agreed Roberto, nodding. Margo also nodded. "Is it as nice inside as out?"

"I don't know," said Roberto.

"You really haven't been inside before," I asked. "I've never been here at all."

"Oh Christ," I said. "How do you know we're at the right house?" Roberto looked over his shoulder at the imposing house and then turned back to me. "Do you think there might be others?"

"It could be the wrong place. We could get shot on a dark night like this for pounding on the door."

Roberto smiled and then laughed quietly. "We could get shot if it is the right house," he said. "But I don't think we will. I don't think Kathy would let him shoot us. For damn sure she'd never forgive him if he did. She likes me. A lot."

Kathy answered our knock. Her face, strangely, showed no emotion.

She acted as if the inevitable meeting of Roberto and her parents had arrived and she had resigned herself to it. She greeted Roberto almost formally, invited him into the house, and then warmly greeted Margo and me in the same way. Though she had met me only briefly, she accorded me the same reserved warmth that she did Roberto.

Kathy may have been in full love with Roberto. He had told me that many times she had asked Roberto to "call" on her at her Cananea home and to meet her family so that their relationship could attain a higher degree of legitimacy regardless of the fact that Roberto's father and grandfather had worked the Cananea mines. The parents had never met Roberto and probably did not know of his existence. Roberto and Kathy, until this night, were engaged in a strictly geographical love affair. What she wanted was for him to visit her, formally and respectfully, as her parents would require; that is, to get the approval of the family, at least as much as possible. She must have loved Roberto quite strongly to be so desperate that she would accept the formal family introductions under these circumstances. Kathy obviously knew that without the appropriate procedures being followed, their already precarious relationship would be doomed. And she obviously knew that these circumstances stood an exceedingly small chance of succeeding but would likely be the only opportunity.

I felt sorry for Kathy. When Roberto called with the suggestion that all three of us come over for a self-invited visit, Kathy certainly saw disaster. Our generation was a ragged one that ignored normal protocol. Here comes her secret boyfriend on a self-invited thirty minutes notice on a rain-and-wind -

swept dark evening, bringing with him another woman and another man. He comes wrapped in a serape, smelling of tacos and beer. And he comes not for the purposes Kathy hopes for. Roberto and his pals are looking for a dry place to sleep.

We knocked on the huge solid wood door. A bright light and camera greeted us first. Kathy opened the doors to her father's home for us despite the difficulty it would surely cause her. She did not complain to us in any way; she welcomed us into the house as cordially as if these were common, normal circumstances.

From the entrance (that reminded me of a church vestibule), we were led to a small, triangular sitting lounge that preceded a dark living room. In the little sitting room were five stiff-backed chairs and two coffee tables. The walls were brick, and the floor was red tile covered by a woven rug that was most beautiful and probably purchased for far less than it was worth. There were pieces of the art of Latin America on the walls, and I checked my shoes carefully for mud. There was some, but not as much as I feared. Another young woman, who by her looks had to be Kathy's sister, came into the room after we were seated. Her hair was lighter than Kathy's, and she had a smaller frame and was not quite as pretty as Kathy. She was older than Kathy, but not much. To my surprise, Kathy's sister, named Susan, knew Roberto—they greeted each other casually. I was surprised that Susan knew Roberto and figured that the sisters were co-conspirators regarding the rain-and-mud-splattered visitor.

Susan stayed with us only a few minutes, and then she left to get refreshments. Kathy was reserved but polite, speaking to Margo and me as well as to Roberto. Roberto was too quiet for my comfort. Margo was smoking cigarettes, and I could see that she enjoyed watching the awkward exchanges between the presumed lovers. I felt good sitting in the warm house and the dry chair and not being one of the principals of the drama.

Susan returned with a tea tray and teapot. She also had a dozen pieces of fruit bread. When the serving was complete, Susan sat in a seat that tended to cut Roberto and Karen off from the rest of us.

Susan spoke to me. "How are your school holidays going?"

"Fine," I answered, smiling. "I spent the first days with my family." Susan turned to Margo. "Did you also spend your time with your family?"

"No," Margo shook her head. "My family is too far away. They are in Germany."

"Your whole family is in Germany?"

"My whole family is my mother and my son. He is with my family while I am in school in America."

"You have a son?" Susan seemed genuinely surprised. "How old is he?"

"Seven."

"Oh my! That's nice. Don't you miss him?" Margo smiled broadly. She had been down this road before. "Of course. I miss him a great deal, but it was the only way to get this degree."

Susan turned to me. "Do you also have a son?" I could not tell if she was joking.

"No, I'm too young."

"I do," called out Roberto. "He was in California last I heard. His mother took him away when she remarried. I've got to find him one of these days. He's getting to the age where he will need his father."

Susan did not turn to receive Roberto's comment, and no one acted surprised, so I suspected that his child revelation came as news to no one. In a minute, Roberto and Kathy had returned to their conversation.

"Are you a student?" asked Roberto. "Yes, in California. Berkeley." "What do you study?"

"Political science and Spanish."

"Latin American politics?" questioned Margo with a cock of her head.

"No. Latin American diplomacy," Susan answered.

We three were silent for a minute. We could hear Kathy and Roberto talking of events that had occurred in Cananea when they were both children. Now they spoke in English. It seemed that they were struggling for subjects to talk about. It was embarrassing to be able to hear them, like forced eavesdropping. I wished they would return to the privacy of speaking Spanish so that at least Margo and I didn't have to listen. "How long are you staying in Cananea?" Susan asked all of us.

"Two days," answered Margo, too quickly. One thing Margo had never learned in the United States, or anywhere, was to be stingy with the truth. It was true that we intended to stay for two days, but that fact might or might not mean two nights. It was careless of Margo, and we were too close to what we hoped for to be so careless. The thought of guests (if floor-sleepers qualified as guests) for two nights as opposed to one night, with already a quarter passed, is a thought that requires significant benevolence and increases geometrically the nature of the so far hidden request. We were not (as of yet) sucking for such benevolence. I hastened to correct Margo's error.

"We arrived here today. We will probably go elsewhere or even back to Arizona tomorrow." Tomorrow's plan had not been discussed between us, contrary to my implication, but Margo drew enough from my words not to correct me.

Kathy asked, "Where are you staying tonight?"

I knew it would come. I even thought I could again hear the hard rain and its' brother, the cold wind. There was a pause in the conversation of Roberto and Kathy, a pause created by Roberto.

"Well," I began, "we don't really know yet. We were going to camp out, but I'm not sure we'll be able to find any place dry enough. We don't have a tent… no excuse for that."

Susan watched me stumble through my little speech.

"… Do you have any ideas where a dry spot might be on a night like this?" I asked finally.

Susan continued staring at me. I thought the two sisters might be on to us. My little explanation had come out right, not too presumptuous and not too timid, just a reasonable question under the circumstances. I waited for Susan to offer a suggestion. After a long minute, she lowered her eyes from me. "Well, let's see," she said. "Not right offhand, I don't, but give me a minute and I'm sure I'll come up with something."

She wants to discuss it with Kathy before she makes a public offering, I thought. Before too long they would excuse themselves and then return with the idea that we unroll our sleeping bags on the living room carpet. Only a person as cold as the wind would send another person into the wind and the rain that ran amok outside the dry walls of the house.

I began to suspect that the whole affair was heading for an unpleasant crash. We had not seen or heard the parents, and neither sister had made mention of them. Perhaps they were gone for the weekend.

Perhaps Roberto and Kathy would find love if only for a wet and windy night. Perhaps I would find my way to Susan's bed (we had made some good eye contact; she sat closer to me than to Margo and once touched my knee with her hand, ostensibly as a means of explanation). In that case, it would be only Margo on the floor, but she would probably get the guest's bedroom or, at least, a living room couch. For all, there is a time to do without. I felt like Margo's time was fast approaching. Too bad Susan and Kathy didn't have an older brother.

My dreamy desires were immediately dashed by the entrance of the parents. I shouldn't have been surprised. Isn't that how it goes? What can a man do to protect himself against such often -taken revenge when he has permitted his desires to multiply by greedy leaps, unchecked by responsible thought? One, as a man comes in search of a dry place to sleep, everything seems to be going well since his request and his desire are so small and humble. Everything goes so well, in fact, that the young man grabs for more than the original thought. Then, when the man has trapped himself, does revenge come forward to violently twist the apple from the young man's mouth?

Kathy stood when her parents entered the room. Her father smiled and nodded at her as if he had not seen her for a considerable time. The mother, a quiet and somber woman, seated herself in the chair Kathy had vacated, but the mother did not, as far as I could determine, acknowledge Kathy. She did not glance at the rest of us even briefly, when she entered the room or when she was seated. Kathy stood to the side of the chair, against the wall with her hands behind her back, her face still without significant expression.

Kathy's father stood next to the chair for introductions. He was dressed in a fine suit, a knee-length raincoat draped over his arm. His shoes were well shined. The parents were clearly going out for the evening.

The mine president took a step forward toward Roberto and reached to shake hands. "Jack Miller," he announced, shaking Roberto's hand with a slight nod of his head.

"Roberto Ortiz," replied Roberto. After the handshake, Roberto returned to his seat.

Margo was between Roberto and me. When Jack Miller passed in front of her, he paused and smiled, nodded, and repeated his name, but he made no movement to shake hands with her. Margo anticipated his every move and simply mirrored his greeting and remained seated. "Margo," she said and left it at that.

Jack Miller took one more step toward me. I was already on my feet.

He shook hands with me, a powerful shake by him (that was designed to establish dominance). He repeated his name in case I hadn't heard it and granted me the same slight nod he had granted to Roberto. After he said his name, I said mine. Then Jack Miller stood next to the chair where his wife sat, announcing without speaking that the visit would not be moved to the living room, where it could be much more comfortable for everyone. His body language clearly announced that the surprise, uninvited guests would not be around very long.

Determined to get it out and not miss her chance, Kathy spoke quickly. "Daddy, this is Roberto Ortiz, the young man I told you about. He's going to school in Tucson, but he comes from Cananea."

Jack Miller watched Roberto as his daughter spoke. When she finished, he nodded to indicate that he heard her and that he remembered. "Where do you live now, Mr. Ortiz? In Arizona?" Even though 'Ortiz' was the only Spanish word spoken, I could tell that Jack Miller's accent and pronunciation were flawless.

"Yes," answered Roberto, "in Arizona."

"And your family? Do they live in Arizona too?"

"Yes." Roberto used no abundance of words to answer the man, but he had not yet removed his eyes from the man or his hands from under his serape.

"And what are you studying in school?"

"I told you, Daddy," interrupted Kathy. Neither man paid attention to the interruption.

"Latin American History and Law," answered Roberto.

Mr. Miller nodded. I had been watching him carefully. He was at absolute ease. He was between forty-five and fifty, though he was in good physical shape and could pass for thirty-five. The skin on his face was tight, his eyes were clear, and his hair was short and light. The man did not smile much, but from the little he did, I noted that his teeth were perfect.

The mine president continued with Roberto. "Did any of your relatives work in the mine here?" The question seemed inevitable. "All of them," answered Roberto. "How goes the mine?"

Jack Miller nodded. "The mine goes fine. We expect this to be our most productive year."

Suddenly the man ended the conversation by turning to Margo. He was in complete control.

"What do you do?" he asked her. "I'm also a student."

"Do you have a family in Arizona with you?"

"My son is with my mother in Germany until I get through with school."

"You have only a son?"

"I have no daughter."

"Only a son in Germany then?"

"I don't have a husband either. I used to, but no more."

"And so you just travel around with these two young men?" Jack Miller's finger came out from under his coat and pointed first to Roberto and then to me. Margo was taken back but she recovered quickly. I heard Kathy take a deep breath, more like an objection.

"For a few days," Margo said calmly. "It's school break this week. They are my friends."

"Oh," said the mine president. "You would rather have a profession than be with your son and your family?"

"Oh, Daddy." Sighed Kathy.

"It's alright," said Margo, looking Mr. Miller straight on without blinking. "I have both," she said proudly.

The mine president developed a sarcastic grin and finished that segment of the 'get to know you' conversation. I was amazed at how pleasantly Margo was able to calmly answer the man, and I wondered if I would be as calm as she had. The mine president used only body language to express his disbelief that Margo was what or who she said she was. Then he turned to me.

"And where are you from? We seem to have a regular United Nations here."

Before I could answer, it was easy to catch the moans of the mine presidents' daughters. The mother/wife did not speak or move or reveal her feelings. I chose to respond directly and politely to keep this party alive.

"I'm from Arizona."

"Always Arizona?" he asked.

"I was suckled on it." I hadn't known I was going to say that, but when I saw Roberto laugh and Margo chuckle, I was glad I had. Jack Miller smiled, which I was thankful for given that I was still holding out hope for a dry place to sleep. I quickly followed up. "I've always lived there," I said, in an awkward attempt to convert back to the formal.

"So it would seem if you were suckled on it."

"That's just an expression," I explained. "An expression my uncle used all the time."

"Oh." Jack Miller was finished with me. He glanced at the three of us. "How long are you boys going to be here?"

"At least two days," answered Roberto.

Unlike Margo's attempt to answer truthfully, Roberto answered more as a challenge than an answer. *The cat's out of the bag now,* I thought.

"Have you boys taken rooms in town?" asked Jack Miller.

Before Margo or I could form a proper answer to this delicate question, Roberto answered. "No, we plan to camp," he said defiantly. So Roberto got his defiance, and we lost any chance of sleeping dry on the floor of the mine president's home. The mine president smiled, happy to hear the answer and happy to think of us camping in the rain and mud.

"It's quite wet out, I believe," was all Jack Miller said.

"And muddy," added Roberto. He looked down at his shoes and checked them closely and then looked directly at Father Miller. "I don't think we dragged any mud in." The two men silently watched each other until I thought the air between them would break.

Karen broke the stiff silence. It was easy to sense her discomfort. "Daddy, can you think of any place where they might stay dry on a night like this?"

Mr. Miller lowered his head to think about the question posed by his daughter. Kathy remained standing against the wall and was expressionless. The wife and mother contributed nothing to the query. "Well, let me see now. There is a thick grouping of trees several miles down the road that might have a spot of dry ground under them if the wind isn't blowing too hard." Jack Miller motioned to the dark side of his house. "It's not much of a road that way, though. Unless you have a Jeep, I wouldn't try it. You might get stuck."

"We could take them in our Jeep," suggested Karen, her voice breaking.

"No, you don't," said her father with his most strenuous voice. There was a mixture of anger and exaggerated concern. He looked from one daughter to the other to be sure each got his message. "You are absolutely not to go down that road on a night like this. It is very dangerous."

"Well, we should go," said Jack Miller after a minute. He tapped his wife's shoulder. "We have a dinner engagement," he explained to us. "Sorry I don't have more time to visit with you; perhaps another time." Well, I thought, that's that. We had no room in town, and we had no floor with a roof over our heads. The rain and the wind still came hard; a cold December rain and wind when the nights are at their longest and the night promised to be the longest of the year, maybe the longest of our lives. Oh well, it could be survived. If nothing else, we could sit up in the tiny car and drink tequila and talk and drink more until the night passed with a record number of lies and exaggerations being told. It would be told as an adventure in the future. We would laugh about it months and years later, the three of us, more so than if the night had passed in dryness and comfort; the wild was always better fabric for memories than the ordinary.

Now that the elders were gone, I was content to stay as long as possible and in that way shorten the night, that is, to steal from darkness a piece of the misery it held in store for us. Between the three of us, we could have come up with the cost of a basic Mexican room, but none of us was willing to admit failure, at least not yet. But it was not long, not nearly long enough for me, before there was discussion about where the three of us might be staying that night. The sisters and Roberto outlined the possibilities for Margo. I stayed silent—there was nothing I could add.

Finally, Susan, lost love of my night, came up with what she considered a possibility. "Hey Kathy, do you think the old Yaqui shack would work? It's probably a real mess, but I think it still has a roof and walls."

Karen was frowning and was clearly ready to reject the idea as ridiculous when Roberto spoke up. "Where's the Yaqui Shack?" There was interest in his voice.

"In the hills," Susan answered, but still her eyes were on Kathy, trying to discern what her sister thought of the idea.

"What hills?" asked Roberto.

"Behind the mine's slag piles west of town. I'm sure you must have gone into those hills with your friends when you lived here."

Roberto nodded. "Yea, we used to run around out there. But the only shack I remember belonged to an old Yaqui couple who knew sorcery, and everyone was afraid of them."

"That's them," said the sisters at the same time. "They died about six months ago."

"They both died?" said Roberto.

"On the same day we heard," answered Susan. "Everyone said they were born on the same day and died the same day."

"That's flat-out spooky," said Margo.

"Who owns the shack?" I asked. Both sisters shrugged. "Probably nobody owns it," said Roberto. "Well, maybe the Yaqui tribe owns it, but no Yaqui would live there under the circumstances." I could see that the whole crazy idea of the Yaqui shack appealed to him, and that made me more than a bit nervous.

Susan added more details. "A Yaqui/Mexican man lives at the bottom of the hill, and he farms a pitifully small piece of land. That's all I know."

"Does the farmer own the shack?" asked Margo.

Roberto took a deep breath of frustration. "Nobody owns it. They are Indians, not Americans. Like I said, it's probably owned by the tribe." Kathy discounted everyone. "He's just an old farmer who lives at the bottom of the hill. He's got some goats and crops. Not much."

"How does he guard it?" I asked.

"They say he checks up on it periodically to see that no one vandalizes it."

"Not a problem then," said Roberto. "We're not vandals. We just want to get out of the rain."

"But how will he know that?" I asked.

Again, Roberto showed frustration. "People know such things in Mexico, especially if you're an Indian. This isn't America, where everybody suspects the worst of everyone else." Roberto returned to Karen and Susan.

"Do you know what language they speak?"

Both Kathy and Susan shook their heads. They did not know. But that did not matter to Roberto. "Let's go," he said. The matter was settled in Roberto's mind. He stood, ready to go. When no one else moved, he looked at Margo and me. "Well," he said impatiently. Margo ignored him, addressing herself to Kathy. "Does this shack have a roof?" Shack was the type of word that Margo spoke deliberately, as if she was still speaking a foreign language. It made you think that she was emphasizing the word to figure out just what might be waiting for her. Kathy nodded her head. "I haven't been out there for a long time."

"There used to be a sort of a roof."

Now Roberto looked at me. I threw my hands up to indicate that it was OK by me, even though I wouldn't know if it was OK by me until I saw it, and that would probably be too late.

Roberto turned to Kathy. We had been talking about a place that none of us knew anything about, including where it was, so Roberto's next words were quite predictable, directed at Kathy. "Will you show us where the Shack is?"

Kathy turned to her sister. They talked about the request for only a minute, then concluded that their father had only outlawed driving on the jeep trail in back of the house, and therefore they could justify driving the dirt road (now mud) to the hiking trail that led to the shack, which was in another direction altogether.

Part Three:
In Search of a Haunted Shack That Was Dry

I

The sisters removed the jeep from the protection of the garage.

Rather than being an open, military-type jeep, this was a wagon, fully enclosed and saved from the rain. We rode in Margo's car, following the jeep and the sisters down the muddy road. Roberto drove. I worried the sisters would get the jeep muddy, which was certain, and then have to explain the mud to their father. *Maybe they knew how to handle him,* I thought.

"I can't believe we weren't offered a place on the floor or even in the garage," I said.

Margo snorted. "At the very minimum," she said.

Roberto laughed deeply. He was having a lot of fun. "The garage is huge. It would have been fun in there. I bet Karen and Susan would have sneaked in to play with us. That's why we weren't even offered a garage."

"My family always had room for guests," I said. "And breakfast in the morning."

"Aye." Nodded Margo. "We had an apartment in Berlin, and with that we were lucky. Still, there were people sleeping in the chairs and on the floor more nights than not."

"All someone had to do at our house," I explained, "was to show up and say the name of someone in our family like a password."

"You two are ridiculously naive," said Roberto. He shrugged his shoulders and frowned.

"It's not naive to expect hospitality," said Margo.

"You can't invite yourself into their home," argued Roberto, "not into the home of the president of the mine."

"Well, I don't give a damn about them one way or the other," I said. "Let's drink some tequila."

Roberto smiled. "Well, open the bottle." He smiled. He held a finger up, and he wore the most happy-go-lucky expression I'd ever seen from him. "I'll show you how to drink tequila Mexican style."

"You do that," said the American.

"I'm ready as soon as you put a lime in for me," said the German.

Several miles from town, the exact opposite direction from the mine president's house, was a narrow, winding, and muddy path as dark as the gods could make it. We followed the jeep's taillights for about twenty-five minutes. The so-called road deteriorated with each turn, but before it had failed altogether, it came to a stop and ceased to exist. The rain had stopped, and the clouds were extremely low, beginning to break the sky apart. The wind, still very strong, was pushing the clouds through the sky just above the hilltops as if there was a frantic race to get to another place. The moon broke through when the clouds parted in front of where they had been stationed. It was very bright and provided plenty of light to hike by.

Margo, Roberto, and I strapped our packs to our backs and started down the so-called trail, led by Kathy and Susan. Shortly we saw a small, humble dwelling surrounded by a fence of trees. The dwelling had no lights on. The word passed through our ranks and was finally received by me that this dwelling was that of the man who guarded the shack that was our destination. We all took pains to pass by the dark dwelling in silence, although, with the wind as our cover, there was not much need for furtiveness.

We walked a well-beaten trail that was certainly the trail of the Yaqui couple who once resided in these hills. When the moon came out from behind the clouds, I could see stands of trees dotting the landscape in ravines and washes, but the predominant feeling was open and naked. It was open and vulnerable to the light of the moon, to the strength of the wind, and to the harshness of a December rain. There existed a rawness and lack of protection that made the storm that enclosed us seem much more powerful.

After climbing, though not steep, we came to slag piles that held not one tree or other scrap of vegetation. The slag piles were shaped as barren sand or snow. I wondered where the mine itself was. I wondered if there might be abandoned shafts that we could stumble into in the dark. I wondered if the entire mountain we were on was a mountain of copper deposits and waste. I wondered if we might be banished from the mountain, somehow, by the spirits of the Yaqui couple.

After climbing the slag piles and tailings, we again walked on a trail of beaten earth. We walked level for another thirty minutes before coming to a place where the trail climbed steeply under the bright moon. I could see a spot that would put us between two soft peaks, a spot that held the shack.

The shack sat so very alone on that small spot of flat earth. The far side of the shack was where everything flowed, where all movement came from, and where the shack would slide away if it chose to do so. In the darkness and in the fleeting light of the moon, I could see that the tiny hut existed without mercy. All sight and sound was funneled into a darkness that had no bottom, and still the shack stood in defiance of the suction that pulled everything else into its' darkness.

The shack was built of sheet metal skirted around a rotten wood frame. The unpainted metal, partly rusted, dully reflected the moon. The metal roof was of square metal sheets held down by heavy boulders.

Despite the boulders, the corners of the metal sheets frequently lifted enough to slap the other metal sheets. Never before had I seen anything more lonely than the dark square of metal pitted against all the elements.

The door to the shack was nonexistent, and the windows had no screen or glass if they ever had any. The first room was about five feet by seven feet but had no interior walls, only rusting metal of different dimensions.

The floor had once been boarded, but that job had been constructed on raw earth without the benefit of any kind of foundation. The three -inch -wide floorboards had buckled at forty-five-degree angles and were damp; rank earth oozed up between all boards. Against one wall was a metal spring bed frame absent a mattress. A faded mirror with a deep brown matrix hung adjacent to the bed frame. In the frame of the mirror was inserted a host of religious pictures depicting Jesus, the Virgin of Guadalupe, and some of the apostles. Of Jesus, there were several renderings. A black rosary was hung around the mirror's frame. In a corner, below the mirror, Karen picked up a figurine of the Virgin of Guadalupe.

The right plaster arm was broken at the shoulder. Roberto still held the flashlight. I stood behind him as he searched the other areas of the shack. It did not take long. In the corner was a large potbelly stove, but no wood. There was a window frame with no window in it. There was a kerosene lamp with about a third of an inch of brownish kerosene still in the bowl.

The wick did not reach the level of the kerosene. I adjusted the wick to soak up what was left of the fluid.

"What do you think?" asked Karen, finally breaking the silence. "It will keep you dry, don't you think?"

"Certainly," answered Roberto. "It will be a dry place to sleep." There was no emotion in his voice, and I could not see his face.

"I hope the roof doesn't leak." Susan had the light. She was examining the underside of the roof.

"Is there any wood in the stove?" asked Margo. I took the light to check. There was none. It was very wet inside. "No," I called to Margo.

"But you have good sleeping bags, right?" said Susan.

"Yes," Roberto answered as if he'd already answered ten times.

"I wonder if there are rats in here," said Margo.

"No rats," I answered. "If anything, it would be shrews. Rats need garbage to keep them going."

"No rats, no shrews, no garbage, and no leaking, got it everybody?"

said Roberto, getting more frustrated with all the questions. He tossed his gear on the steel bed frame. "Everything will be fine."

"Have you got the lantern working?" Susan asked me.

"Yes," I said and lit the lantern.

"We can take the flashlight back with us then?" asked Susan.

"Of course… you'll need it for the trail back," said Roberto as if he was trying to move them along.

When I had the kerosene lamp burning and hung on a wall, there was silence save the wind. Karen suggested that she and Susan go. There was no life in her words. She came to Roberto and gave him a kiss. Roberto did not respond with any detectable passion. We said good-bye and thanked them for their assistance, and then they left without ceremony. We did not speak for some time after they left, and it was strange how long you could hear them, picking their way along the trail, giving instructions and warnings to each other.

"They didn't stay long, did they?" I said after I was sure that the sisters were out of hearing range.

"No, of course not," answered Roberto. Margo did not respond. She was looking for a place to unroll her bag and claim a space. I was glad that neither Roberto nor Margo responded to my comment. It was a stupid thing to say in the first place. I didn't want to stay long either. It was a violation, and I could feel it. I didn't know if my friends felt it, but I suspected they did. Even though we lived in an era of irreverence, we should respect fear in the soul when it speaks to us and tells us we should stay away. Outside the shack, I searched for a place to lay my sleeping bag. The wind, like the moon, came hard at us and then not at all. There was nothing outside the shack except mud and rock. No trees. I went to the lee side of the shack, out of the wind, but a foot of mud occupied that spot.

Suddenly, as I started back, I heard a gunshot from inside the shack and then a second one immediately following. I heard Margo scream. The gunshots were the loudest thing in the universe, and it must have been louder inside the shack. I knew immediately who fired the shots and why the shots were fired. I went inside.

Margo stared, white-faced and horror -stricken, at Roberto. Casually he was checking the gun to be certain it was empty. The shattered mirror lay on the floor, and there were two bullet holes in the metal where I had been standing, on the outside, only seconds before the shots.

I tried to be calm. "I didn't know you had a gun," I said.

"I always carry a gun when I travel," said Roberto. His voice betrayed an anger not caused by my question. Still, he was inspecting the gun. "You could feel it?" I asked.

"Yes, of course. Who wouldn't?"

"And it had to be desecrated?"

"Yes."

I shook my head. Margo was beginning to calm down, but in her face I could see that she did not understand and had decided the best thing to do was to stay silent. She watched both of us, shaking her head involuntarily. "This is insane," she mumbled.

"Did it work?" I asked Roberto.

"Did what work?" he said, unconvincingly. "Has the place been thoroughly desecrated?"

"Yea, I suppose so. Sort of. Look at that propaganda," Roberto said, pointing to the scattered religious pictures with the gun.

"Yes? I'm looking at it. What about it?"

"It has kept my people in bondage for too many centuries."

"I guess that's your view," I said and was ignored.

“Even up here,” said Roberto. “Even up here and even these people; full-blooded Indians. They weren’t even Mexicans.”

“No,” I said. “They weren’t. They didn’t live in the city.”

“They were probably about twenty years old when the revolution began,” said Roberto. He was shaking his head.

“Yes.”

“And very old by the time it ended,” he continued.

“And probably very old times too when they died,” added Margo. “Could we go to sleep now? You scared the shit out of me. I’m not in the mood to listen to your political diatribe. I’ve got my own diatribe. I don’t have a gun to start with, like you do. I want the so -called bed to sleep on.”

Roberto looked behind him to where his gear rested on the naked steel webbing of the bed. “I’ve got the bed,” said Roberto.

“Take the goddamn thing then… It’s your country; you take the bed.”

Margo started to unroll her bag next to the bed on the floor. I reached the tequila bottle from my pack, drank, and handed the bottle to Roberto. He drank and handed the bottle to Margo. He had to nudge her with the bottle to get her to take notice.

“Here!” He raised his voice a bit with a touch of frustration.

“I don’t want any,” answered Margo. “Drink some, Goddamn it!” Now the frustration had a bite to it. “I don’t want any, Goddamn it,” said Margo with her own bite. “Drink some anyway,” insisted Roberto. “We’re in this together.”

Margo sighed and took the bottle. “I suppose I’ll need it anyhow to get some sleep. This place is probably haunted.”

We sat drinking the tequila and smoking but not talking. Roberto sat on the bed frame. Margo sat cross-legged on her sleeping bag, and I squatted against the doorframe. We passed the bottle, each sipping in turn. Now I could see Margo. When the bottle was passed to her, she drank, but tiny amounts, about a thimbleful.

The waste from my cigarettes; the ashes, the burnt matches, and the butts were a problem for me. Roberto and Margo used the damp dirt floor between the pushed-up boards. There was not much choice unless you wanted to get up and go to the door or the window each time the ash grew. Still, I could not use the floor as they did for fear that it would be seen as a further violation; instead, I deposited them into my hand and, when cool, into my shirt pocket. The matches and the butt I placed in the pocket of my jeans when they were cool and dead. I was wary of spirits that might be silently present.

After we had passed the bottle about a dozen times, Margo started passing it without drinking. Roberto and I had a few more turns at the bottle and another cigarette each, and then Roberto stepped over Margo and went outside of the shack.

"What do you think?" I asked her. "What do I think about what?"

"All of this."

"Not a hell of a lot."

"Nor do I. Do you think you'll be able to sleep?"

"Sure… if you boys would quiet down and turn the lantern off, I'd be able to sleep, or at least fake it."

"I doubt that I can even fake it."

"Why?"

"After all of this, I just don't see it, but it's not a big deal."

"Well, that's your problem. Don't keep me awake with you."

"No, of course not…how is it on the floor."

"It feels like a washboard."

Roberto returned and started to prepare his bed for sleeping. With Margo stretched out parallel to the bed, there was only room enough for my bag next to the door. Once we thought we were settled, Roberto started talking.

"Hey, Stewart," he said, laughing. "If the old man who guards this place comes up here with his shotgun, you'll be the first person he meets, no?" He indicated the position of my bag next to the door with his head and a grin.

"If I was in the bag when he came up here with a shotgun, that would be true. But I'm not getting in that bag. So if he comes, I'll be awake and I'll show, him where you are and tell him you're the one who fired shots up here."

"Do that," said Roberto. "And be sure to tell him my name."

"I will."

The lantern went dim and then out. I could not retrieve the light.

"Don't go to sleep yet," I called to Roberto, though I could no longer see him. Actually, I didn't want to go to sleep. I wanted to stay awake in case something happened or someone did come. I wanted to be prepared. "Let's drink some more tequila," I said.

"I don't want any more," said Roberto.

"Both of you shut up and go to sleep," said Margo.

I smoked a cigarette and drank small amounts from the bottle. Still, there was plenty of tequila left. I thought I'd lost both of them for the night when Roberto spoke out.

"Do we have any kerosene left in the lantern?"

"No, just a few drops at the bottom of the bowl." I answered. "Enough to start a fire?"

"Maybe if you started your fire with something really dry and small and went on from there. The wick is still damp with kerosene."

"I do have something to burn. I think we should burn this place to the ground, Stewart."

I chuckled and said, "And then where would we sleep?"

"That doesn't matter. It's only for one night, but this place would be gone forever. Hand me the lantern."

I did not do so. "I'm certain that this place wouldn't burn."

"The frame would," he said.

"Yes, but not the sheet metal."

"With the frame consumed, the rest would fall down on top of itself." "And then it would be a monument," I said.

Roberto did not say anything for a minute. I heard him turn over in the steel bed and take a deep breath that signaled to me that he was going to say something that he considered important. And then he did. "I considered hunting that man," he said. From the sound of his voice, I could tell that he was facing the metal, not me. "What, man?" I asked.

"The mine President, Kathy's father, Jack Miller."

"And why would you do that?" I asked calmly.

"I don't know…A thousand reasons… My father died in that mine, you know."

For a minute, I said nothing. All of a sudden, everything was changed. "No, I didn't know. Was it an accident?"

"Naturally they said it was an accident but there are no accidents in the mine."

"How old were you."

"When?"

"When you considered Jack Miller's future."

Roberto laughed. "Tonight I considered it when we were at their house."

"Tonight!" I yelled. "Yes."

Margo was definitely not asleep. "Oh God," she moaned. "What the hell is all of this shit?"

Roberto chuckled. "Of course I did. The anger was under my serape."

"Jesus Christ!" is all I could say.

Roberto laughed at me. He was still facing the metal. "I changed my mind when I met him."

"Well, I'm glad for that," I said. "What made you change your mind?"

"I saw in his eyes how much he hated and feared me."

"Jesus Christ, man," I said. "You're not talking sense. Come over here and drink tequila with me."

Margo was moaning her disgust, not taking it seriously.

"No," said Roberto. "I am serious. He hated me. He hates me. He knows I've had his daughter, and he knew who I was and where I came from, and he knew how dangerous I am to him and his daughter."

"So?" I said, trying not to get too worked up.

"So to hate and to fear is a very painful thing. It was fun to watch.

I'd rather stretch it out."

After a few seconds of silence I said, "I see. You let him suffer with hate and fear?"

"That's right. But he'll hate more before he's done living. That's the real reason I changed my mind."

"How's that?" I asked, a bit worn out with the conversation.

"When his mine is taken away by those he despises, he'll hate twice as much. He has spent his whole life with it. It is his life, but he will live to see it taken away from him by those he hates."

"So now you've spared him so he could live to see this come about?"

"To see it and feel it." Roberto swung himself into a sitting position on the bed. His hand came out of the dark and took the tequila from me. I could hear him drink deeply. The metal webbing under him complained.

He laughed and said, "Good night, Stewart; good night, Margo." Margo said, basically to herself, *"Men are such idiots."*

And then I was alone. I didn't know if Roberto Ortiz meant what he said. I knew Roberto well enough to know that he was a master of making statements that could not be verified or refuted. I was struck by the absence of a visceral voice telling me how much truth existed in what he had said. I felt completely ignorant of whether my friend was deadly serious or stringing me along in order to expand his precious reputation. It was the oddest of feelings, sitting in the dark shack that could very well be inhabited by the spirits of peasant Indians and not knowing. As these thoughts were consuming me, Roberto spoke again. "And the next thing I'm going to do for Mr. Miller will be very pleasurable. I'm going to get Kathy pregnant. His grandchild will be a filthy cross-breed."

Before Margo could explode, I reached over and rubbed her back and whispered to her, "Don't bother; we just need to ride this out."

The wind blew very hard. Inside the shack was black and creaking loudly. Only when the clouds unveiled the moon did the faintest bit of light come back to the shack. Under ordinary circumstances, I am a lover of storms, but this storm raged; these were not even close to ordinary circumstances. As far as I was concerned, this storm screamed from the bowels of the earth and from the souls of the world's peasants. The wind could not decide if it should blow without end or come in vicious bursts so that the rain could pound us into infinity.

It was I who stayed the night with the storm. Violation, invasion, and desecration had occurred, and revenge could be expected in some form. Who is to know the time and form revenge might take. Revenge is silent with but one goal, one purpose assigned it in the universe. The task is retribution, matching a serious wrong for a wrong, a theft with a loss, a wound inflicted with an injury received, greed unashamed filled with a time of famine, oppression caused with oppression suffered? Does revenge care a damn for swiftness suffered? Not really; memory is sibling to revenge and revenge, takes a sweet course.

My friends were fast asleep, and I could hear their deep, regular breathing. I had the tequila between my legs as my only assistant. Sometime during the night, I took to chanting, chanting single syllables in low, melodic tones. The chanting had a soothing effect, and when my mouth grew dry from the chanting and from the cigarettes, I drank tequila. At one point, I started to talk to no one. I spoke about a lot of things having nothing to do with the shack or the wind and rain. It was the act of speaking what was valuable, not the substance of the words.

The wind continued to rage, and the clouds continued to speed past the moon in huge chunks like icebergs. Late into the night, about an hour before morning's first light, it started to rain hard again. Then came lightning and thunder with a show of power that made my soul quake. I squatted further down and pulled myself into myself as much as possible, frozen, but never did I take my eyes from the outside of the shack. It was the lightning that concerned me most. At one point, there was everything the storm could throw. The wind screamed like the roar of ten thousand peasants; the muted light of the moon mocked me; the rain beat the earth and shack furiously; lightning followed by thunder imprisoned me. I could not move my body, and my eyes, unblinking, were focused on anything foreign.

Eventually the elements subsided, one by one. First went the rain, and then the lightning followed by its shadow, thunder. The clouds broke into smaller pieces and slowed their torrid pace across the sky. The wind began a slow, unsatisfied retreat into the abyss. And finally, the moon started giving way to the first light of day. I knew what I'd seen was nothing; it was merely a cynical acknowledgment of my vigil but not, certainly not, a forgiveness. No price had been set or extracted. With temporary calm and light, I was able to go to my sleeping bag.

The bag was wet inside from dampness in the earth that had soaked through the floor and into the bag. I kept my clothes on, and though I could feel the wet, I was asleep before it could bother me.

In less than two hours, I was awakened by Roberto and Margo. The sky was clear with a bright, warm sun. When I got outside, into the sun, Roberto and Margo laughed at me. I must have been a mess.

"How did the night go, Stewart?" asked Roberto.

"Fine," I said.

"You look terrible," said Margo. "You look like you stayed up all night."

"No, nothing like that," I said. "I'm fine."

"Did you drink all the tequila yourself?" Roberto held up the nearly empty bottle.

I shook my head. "The old Yaqui man that once lived here had some."

Both laughed quietly. "When did the storm stop?" asked Margo.

"It didn't," I said.

We walked down the hill and past the slag piles. At the house at the bottom of the hill, fenced in by ocotillo, where the rumored guard lived, we came upon a man leaning against an old shovel. Roberto talked to the man in Spanish for a while, and I stood by mute and somewhat embarrassed by my lack of any language beyond English. After the Yaqui spoke for a while with Roberto (obviously the man was fluent in both of his native languages, Yaqui, and in Spanish) he politely turned to me and asked me something in Spanish that I did not understand at all. Assuming the friendly man was greeting me, I said, "Buenos dias, senior." After we had walked about ten yards away, Roberto looked at me, somewhat disgusted. "You should have at least made an effort to talk with the man," he said. And he was serious. Though he knew I spoke not more than thirty words of Spanish, he insisted that I should have made an effort to speak Spanish with the man. Odd as it seemed, I did not argue with him and even thought that perhaps I should have tried. But it would have been ridiculous.

In town, we bought sugar rolls from a bakery and small cartons of milk from a nearby store. Roberto did the talking. The bakery was across the street from the town's plaza. A lot of the kids were practicing the procession to the church for their first communion. On our side of the plaza were twenty girls, all about seven years old, all dressed in white dresses and veils. Across the plaza was a like number of boys the same age, dressed in dark suits, their dark hair combed neatly back and shining in the morning sun. We sat on the curb in front of the bakery to eat our breakfast and to watch the procession. The children looked around self-consciously, as they paraded with pride in their eyes and a great deal more in the faces of their onlooking parents.

In the early afternoon, we returned to the bar where we had been the day before and reclaimed our seats. There were only a few patrons who did not smile. We each drank beer, and by late afternoon, Roberto and Margo were feeling pretty good. I had a vague feeling that had not yet firmed itself into a desire or conviction, but I wasn't ready to return to the United States; I wanted to slip out the back door, deeper into Mexico or beyond, Central America or even South America. I didn't think too much about it, and with drinking beer, I was unable to form any resolutions.

Besides, I couldn't even speak Spanish.

"We could stay another night at the shack," I said all of a sudden.

"It's not raining anymore." I was as surprised as Roberto and Margo were at my suggestion. Even so, something tugged at me; something wanted to go back to the shack.

Margo said, "It's a hell of a walk in the dark."

"Not me," said Roberto. "That shack doesn't mean anything to me."

I knew before I had made the suggestion that it would not happen. A simple stall or delay would do me no good. I resigned myself to the fact that I would not be able to alter the experience of the previous night at the shack. I resigned myself to the fact that I'd failed to share a night with a Yaqui couple who probably lived their entire life farming the land and living in the shack and had learned what I would never know. Maybe Roberto and Margo already knew what I was still looking for, or maybe not.

Outside on the street, it was growing dark. The men we passed on the street stood still to examine Margo, but none of us paid any attention to the men. When we were near the car, I noticed that Margo was staring at me.

"You don't look well, Stewart," she said. Her face wrinkled as she squinted to get a better look at me. "Do you feel all right?"

"Sure, I'm fine," I said, though I did feel strange; not ill, but strange. "You haven't had much to say today."

I shrugged. "There wasn't much to talk about today."

"No, but you've been unusually quiet. Ordinarily you have something to say about everything. You're a little sad-looking too. Are you sure you're OK?"

"Yes, I'm sure."

Margo turned to Roberto but kept her eyes on me as if she did not want me to escape. "He doesn't look well, does he?"

"No, he does not," agreed Roberto with a grin.

"What do you think is up with him?" said Margo.

"It could be tequila," said Roberto. "He had a lot last night."

"I'm fine," I insisted, but they paid no attention to me.

"He did drink a lot, didn't he?" said Margo.

"More than his share, I'd say," said Margo. Roberto agreed. "Maybe it was something he ate," said Margo, smiling to Roberto.

"Could be," said Roberto. "Or it could be the water, or both. The water can get a gringo real easy."

After they had diagnosed me, they left me alone. In truth, I did not feel good, but I did not believe it had anything to do with food or drink or sleep.

It was more of a fear or an apprehension that sits in the pit of your stomach and chews at you from the inside. This was something I could not describe to my friends. The two of them still stared at me as in a dream.

Margo looked straight into my eyes and laughed. When she spoke, it was Roberto she was addressing, not me. "I know just how he feels. I felt that way myself a lot of times."

"En Verdad, I know how he's going to feel; it gets worse before it gets better," said Roberto, now laughing.

"Muy Malo," he said. APROXIMADAMENTE NUMERO 54.

The train leaves Nogales, Arizona, at five o'clock. Be at the train station by four. Go through customs at the train station, or you'll have to do it twice. Don't ask why. Pay two dollars (U.S.) for the tourist card. Never mind that the card says it's free of charge. This is another kind of charge. Tell them you're a professional, not a worker. Go first class. Go primera especial.

It's winter break. You just want to see some of Mexico's pyramids.

Like Teotihuacan in Mexico City and maybe Monte Alban in Oaxaca. You want to travel among the people and discover their culture; experience their world. Travel alone with a single backpack. You cross the frontier at two-thirty so you won't be late. You use the public bathroom, which you now hope you'll be able to mostly avoid. The train station is three miles away. You still have to go through customs and buy your ticket, and they said to be there by four. Three miles is too far to walk and still make it by four. You see a taxi-man and he's calling out in English, "Taxi, taxi?" You know enough to set the price before you get in the car. "How much?" you ask.

"One U.S. dollar," he says.

You can see that the Mexico side of Nogales is a wretched town, but you know what they say; they say you've got to get away from the border towns before making any judgments or drawing any conclusions. They say all border towns are wretched. "What time does the train leave?" you ask your driver.

"Five o'clock," he answers.

"How long to Guadalajara?" you ask.

"One or two days, it depends," he answers.

"Depends on what?" you ask.

"On how fast the train goes," he answers.

Pretty good English, you think.

Your driver pulls up to a driveway underneath the train station, and you hand him a U.S. dollar. You hear him laugh, just as he did when he made the joke about how fast the train goes, and he says, "This isn't five dollars." You think five dollars gets me across Denver. You say, "No, it's not; you said one dollar U.S."

"No, five dollars, you are wrong." You see men in uniforms by the door, but you don't know what the uniforms mean. To your surprise, they ignore you. So you get out of the taxi without paying the driver another penny.

But you are followed into the train station by the taxi-man, and he is yelling at you all the way, demanding, "Five dollars, five dollars!" You see that he has attracted a crowd of children, and these urchins stare at you with strangely mature, worldly, and hostile eyes. But you ignore the taxi-man; you've already paid the agreed-upon amount. A bargain is a bargain.

None of the uniforms seem to be willing to assist the taxi-man in his efforts to extort such a ridiculous charge from you, so you've let yourself feel relieved until you feel a rough grasp on your shoulder and you see an undersized and overcompensating military or police officer pushing a badge in your face and forcing you to follow him.

So you have no choice but to follow him and the taxi-man (who seems to know right where he's going) to a windowless room on the basement floor where there are two more enforcement officers. The doors are locked, and they demand nine dollars or jail; either way is fine with them. You do try to tell them that the taxi-man was demanding four dollars, not nine, before they arrived. They smile. They say it's nine now.

So you pay, but only after you've once again told your side of the story through an interpreter who may or may not be interpreting accurately.

You pay with two five-dollar bills; no one has change. You go back to your place in the ticket line, and one of the enforcement officers takes you to the front of the long line and tells the cashier to give the American friend a primera especial ticket to Guadalajara and also to give him one of the best seats. The cashier looks at the officer and asks, "Aproximadamente numero 54?"

The officer smiles. "Perfecto," he answers.

You pay the cashier for the ticket, but his attention is on other cashiers who are trading jokes and laughing very hard, which makes you worry that your cashier won't get you the right ticket. The cashier takes your money. And you pay two dollars more to a fat man for the tourist card that says right on it in four languages that the card is free. And you get on the train. You feel like you've been kicked in the ass. Of course it's too late when you discover that the ticket master has sold you a first-class regular ticket instead of primera especial, which means you'll be going one or two days (depending, of course, on how fast the train goes) in a second-class car. You notice that the ticket has a seat number (54), but a man is in your seat, so you show him your ticket and point to the seat number, but he only looks at you and shrugs. Everyone in your car is watching to see what you'll do. You do nothing.

Three teenage girls giggle, and the man in your seat smiles at the girls proudly, boastfully. You have to sit next to a fat woman who stinks of tequila and corn. You can only stand for so long until you have to get up and walk around, and you decide to go to the dining car, but you find the door is locked, open only to the Pullman, and the primera especial passengers. The boldest of the teenage girls has occupied your (new) seat while you were gone. When you realize this, you also realize that the entire car is watching to witness what will happen, but the girl departs amid the protests from her friends as you approach. You laugh with the rest at the little joke, but you know you laugh alone. The fat woman sprays you with the smell of tequila and corn. She has the most embracing laugh of all.

She offers you tequila from the bottle, but you shake your head, "No…no gracias."

You know you're not supposed to drink the water, but you think you might, but not on the train because it would be a terrible place to be sick, on a train, for one or two days; more likely two days the way the train crawls and stops at every peasant's hut, you think. So you drink the beer, and it's not cold, and it's terribly overpriced and you're the only one to buy beer; no one else can afford the price that is charged, but you think you need something since you can't drink the water. You see pigs and goats and chickens everywhere; possibly the world's best argument to become a vegetarian, but then you think, no, that's not fair, it's just your current mood speaking. Here, though, they peck and scratch among the litter just as the pigs root out morsels from the litter and garbage piles and just as the goats eat off of the top layer. You can't help but notice that. And you can't help but notice the cows wandering around. Who owns those cows anyway, you say to yourself. So maybe you should be really careful about the food you eat too. So you can't eat the food, especially when the train stops in the villages and the peasant women vendors are there to sell you homemade food. "Uno mas cerveza," you say to the porter. You can't figure why the train sits in the village so long. En La Zona Portuaria con Marlon Brando, you see it posted and peeling away from the wall of the station, but you doubt the village has a theater. You see that everyone drinks soft drinks. It's so terribly hot.

Coca-Cola, Pepsi-Cola, 7-up, Squirt, Orange Crush. But you can't eat the food. It must be cheap, you think, because the other passengers buy it up by the armful.

You can't sit still forever, even though it seems the train will, so you walk forward to the second-class cars where the third-class passengers congregate. Here's where they bring their chickens and goats, or so you've heard. But it's not so; you see none of that, though you couldn't prove it by the smell. Yet you do see something of interest: a fellow countryman dressed in sandals, and a straw hat, and white cotton shirt, and pants. It's the light hair and the beard that distinguish him. But he fails or refuses to acknowledge you; he's gone native, you see. Yet it is curious to watch the peasants of the car watch you while you watch him. They all want to know what you'll say or what you think; they know what they think. But you say nothing, to the faux natives' relief, and you return to your seat. The smell of food is all around you. To her tequila and corn, the fat lady has added a unit of fresh goat's milk cheese. She offers you some, but it is smudged with you don't know what. The train would be a bad place to be sick. Muy mal you say to yourself to practice. You decline the cheese.

You've not peered into the toilet at the back of the car, but you've passed it. You know you'd not be able to stand more than a passing exposure, and you know you couldn't survive nauseousness or worse, or both. You know you can't eat peasant's food or drink the water on the train. But later you can, when you acclimate, you tell yourself. You just need to get through the train ride. Night comes to the train, and everything is changed. No lights are switched on. It is very dark, and soon the people start to fall off to sleep, and you worry because you feel not at all like sleeping, and how will you make it until morning? The unbearable heat abates, but in its place comes the cold of the desert night. The end doors to the car remain open, and the cold air rushes in to chill you. The train is so loud, you notice now, and it screams through the desert, dark and furtive, as if it were passing through a dreadful battle zone. A voice from behind and above you whispers so as not to disturb those who sleep. "A donde va Americano?" You understand the friendly voice's question, but you know that you won't understand the next question because you never learned the language; it was so hard to learn, and you never really needed it.

So you answer, “No comprendo, señor. No hablo espanol.” You hear the man return to his seat, disappointed. A short time later, the porter comes through the car with his bucket of warm beer. The man behind you leans over to speak to you again. “Quiere un cerveza Americano?” So you answer with a sigh, “Si, dos.” The man deals with the porter, and when he informs you of the cost, you note that he’s struck a better price with the beer vendor than you did. You give the helpful man behind you one of the beers. The man thanks you profusely. You cannot see the faces of the other passengers or their eyes, but you wonder if they are judging their compatriot with their expressions; all those who are not asleep, of course.

In the middle of the night, the train pulls into a town larger than a village and makes a stop. What else is new? The loading ramp is jammed with peasants carrying boxes tied with twine and bundles of peasant food to take back to their remote villages. They scurry to the second-class cars when the train stops. Some come into your car but find it full. When the crowd parts, you can see the military men leaning against the white walls, under the lights, dressed in uniforms, and holding automatic rifles. You see them everywhere, soldiers and police, all dressed in special uniforms, all carrying loaded weapons, all looking very much apart from the people. You wonder at such a strong show of force so often, and you wonder if maybe the government doesn’t feel secure, if they feel vulnerable, if they fear the people.

A beggar’s head is in his chest, and his head is covered with a piece of cotton material, leaving only an extended hand as proof that it is a person curled up around a light pole and not a peasant’s forgotten bundle. The beggar is immobile, and you wonder if he is asleep, yet the hand is extended in a humble, begging position. Above the beggar is a worn out movie poster: Ultimo Tango en Paris con Marlon Brando. You see a group of kids on the ramp, all under ten, all shoeless, and you wonder why they are out in the middle of the night instead of home and asleep.

You call one of the kids over to the window, and you give him a ten-peso coin and indicate for him to put the money in the beggar’s hand. You want to see what the beggar does. But the boy you trust the coin to and his friends run off laughing. The man behind you laughs a bit but then stops and says, “No importa, no importa.” So you get off the train, keeping an eye out that it doesn’t leave without you, and buy a beer. You place a five-peso coin in the beggar’s hand and stand back to watch. The hand retracts mechanically, as if switched on by the touch of the coin, into the pile of rags, and then it reappears a second later without the coin. Still you do not see the face of the beggar. The gang of boys returns and follows you around the ramp as you drink your beer, calling and laughing, Tiene diez pesos, Americano? Tiene diez pesos para el mendigo?" And you know their fun is harmless enough, but they draw so much attention to you that you finally decide to re-board the train. You're thankful and surprised that your seat is still vacant. The man behind you indicates that he saved it for you while you were gone, playing with children and beggars. You suppose his price will be another beer.

At dawn, you wonder if maybe you didn't sleep a bit after all. The porter comes through with coffee, and you think the coffee would be all right to drink; it must have been boiled at some stage. You buy a cup, but you cannot drink it because it is too heavily laced with sugar. The heat begins as soon as the sun rises, and now you're by the coast, so the jungle-like humidity is present as well. You think you'll die. But you don't die. You sit in your seat and suffer the heat and humidity, the hunger and weariness, the isolation. You see the distance in kilometers posted on the telephone poles, but it depresses you to see them —it's still so far.

All day you ride like this, having submitted to the condition, insisting to yourself that it's temporary. When darkness comes again, you think you must be almost there. But the train goes on and on and continues to stop in every minuscule village along the way. It's after one in the morning when you pull into Guadalajara. Across the way from the station is a hotel. It's too late to eat you tell yourself. The desk clerk pretends not to understand you at first, then, he searches the register for a long time to see if he might have a room for you. He does, he says, but it's a room for four, with two double beds, so you must pay the price of four if you want the room. You are exhausted. You pay for four. You sort of wish there were four with you.

There is a jug of water in the room. As you came down the hall, you saw big bottles of purified water, but wait; there is no reason to think that the hotel doesn't just refill the bottles with tap water, so you decide not to drink the water in the jug until you've purified it with the tablets you brought along. Then you must wait thirty minutes before drinking the water that you've fixed.

In the morning, you feel better. You get a shower without the promised hot water, and then you go to find a meal. You're starved.

Walking along, you pass several of the city's famous parks and gardens. You find a quaint little restaurant on a side street. You order from the Spanish menu, jugo con huevos. You tell the lady you want the eggs scrambled. Scrambled is your new word in Spanish today. When the order is brought, all the workers are peering at you from wherever they are in the restaurant, hiding their glee and laughter poorly. You are given a large glass of juice with two raw eggs floating in it, not even scrambled. You think calmly that it is too early to succumb. So you drink it down as soon as she hands it to you with one big gulp, like a college drinking binge (although you do struggle a bit when the whole eggs enter your throat).

And then you pay. You do not leave a tip. You leave. They are all laughing. You return to the train station in the afternoon to catch the overnight to Mexico City. You try to buy a primera especial ticket, but they are sold out, or you fail to make yourself understood, or something. You try for a Pullman. No luck. You resign yourself to another journey second-class, but you console yourself with the thought that this trip will not be nearly so long and the heat will not be a factor since you will be traveling at night and at a higher elevation. You shrug and buy a second-class ticket after you've managed to obtain the exact change since the ticket agent refuses to make change for you. And then you wait with your bags for the train's departure because it is many hours late. All the hustlers and beggars approach you, and you wave them off like they are flies. The police and soldiers do nothing but walk around with rifles slung over their shoulders and being sure that they look menacing. Across the main street from the train station is a movie house. El Padrino con Marlon Brando.

But you're right that the train to the Capital is not so bad even though it is still crowded and slow. The air is cool, and darkness is, for some reason, comforting. There is an individual asleep in a seat not far from you, and his shoes are off and the stench is unbearable. You can't believe the smell could be so strong, but there is nothing you can do except breathe through your mouth.

When the sunlight enters the train, you are at the extreme outskirts of the Capital, and you're struck speechless by the slums and the poverty that you pass. Mountains of litter is everywhere and people are mining those mountains of junk. Stagnant ponds of water are choked with trash. Shacks of tin and cardboard push up against the tracks. Raw sewage runs everywhere. Small children smile and wave at the train. The older boys play soccer in fields of broken glass that has punctured the ball multiple times. Older girls work next to their mothers over open fires or huddle in groups wearing ragged dresses. The adults sit next to their shacks and stare with expressions of hopelessness, their hair blown back by the speed of the train passing them by.

In the Capital, you try a taxi once more. The hotel you want is in an extremely awkward part of the city for cars, so the driver insists on letting you out at a major intersection, Insurgentes Y Reforma, which the driver assures you boarders the famous Zona Rosas just a few blocks from your hotel. He does not raise the price on you, but since he cannot change your hundred-peso note, he must keep the change, for he must move his taxi.

The police are insisting, and traffic is building up behind him.

You stand on the sidewalk in the heart of the city that is the soul of the country. The streets are beautiful, wide boulevards, tree-lined with modern buildings and statues and water fountains and theaters.

Apocalipsis Ahora con Marlon Brando. The city as you see it is as beautiful as any that you've seen, but you tell yourself to reserve judgment, that what you see is only a tiny part of the whole and that the rest might be an absolute slum. Nonetheless, you do like what you see; it reminds you of what a Capital should look like, it reminds you of the great cities of your own country. It makes you feel, for the first time since you entered the country, a little bit at home. If your hotel is nearby, then everything should be fine.

You take two steps into the giant park. Suddenly you're pushed violently to the ground from the back. A young man has your wallet. Your backpack is in the young man's possession. You can see the young man running away from you. You see a policeman on the corner not far away but looking in another direction. You scream very loudly at the policeman in your own language. The policeman turns, then sees the thief running away.

You yell that the thief stole your wallet and backpack. The policeman yells at the thief to stop, but he doesn't. You watch the policeman raise his rifle and shoot. He shoots three quick times. You see the thief hit the ground and wiggle his upper body as if he can't move his lower body. All the traffic and all the pedestrians come to a stop. The Capital goes quiet, the sound of the gunshots echoing off the buildings, over and over. Then you see that the pedestrians and the policeman are looking from the fallen thief to you, over and over.

You look at the policeman who has not moved. No one has moved.

The thief is still trying to move, to get up, but he cannot. The policeman has not moved. He looks nervously from the thief to the pedestrians to you and back to the growing crowd of onlookers. And you think you just wanted the thief stopped from taking your property. You only wanted to see the Pyramids. You didn't want this to happen. Most of your money was stashed in your pockets. It wasn't that important. It wasn't so important to you that the thief should have been shot. He's just wiggling but can't get up. You just wanted a little protection for your security. But this is not what you had in mind. A white man's invitation to a Navajo Church It was Gary Paul, Stewart Turner's best friend and a young white man like himself, who invited Stewart to the Indian ceremony. It was Gary Paul who seemed to have adopted the Navajos and their spiritual culture to be his own. His dress was similar, and his speech was minimal with soft-spoken phrases, rarely revealing in his face his inner thoughts or feelings. His hair was naturally black. He wore it long and sometimes plaited into a single, thick braid wrapped tightly with cotton cloth. Stewart was impressed by the ease with which Gary Paul seemed to transcend both worlds and to be accepted comfortably in both worlds, native and white.

The ceremony was to be held beginning on a cool June evening and ending the following morning at sunrise on the reservation forty miles from Flagstaff, Arizona, where Stewart and Gary Paul lived. The ceremony's sponsor was Gary Paul, a great honor that showed the Navajo's acceptance of Gary Paul into their Church. Though Gary Paul had attended other ceremonies since his admission into the Church six months earlier, this was the first in which he would act as sponsor. Gary Paul explained that each ceremony had a sponsor; the sponsor called for a ceremony when they had something in particular, deep within their soul, a seriously troubling affair, that needed purging with the assistance of the Gods and the other Church members and the medicine; the sponsor paid the cost of the ceremony.

Because Gary Paul was the sponsor and had been the one to invite him, Stewart did not feel as inhibited about attending the ceremony as he might have otherwise. For a long time he had wished to attend one of the mysterious peyote rituals, but he did not wish to go where he wasn't welcome or where he'd be resented. Yet even with a sponsor's invitation, after driving the sparse, desperately beautiful forty miles, Stewart felt uncomfortable upon his arrival. The ceremony site was an ancient mud and timber octagon Hogan flanked by at least a dozen pickup trucks and surrounded by a wilderness of nothing but red stone and green ponderosa for twenty miles until the desolate land broke and climbed a sharp, definite cliff face. He heard only an ancient tongue along with the barking of dogs and the laughter of children and the unbroken reservation wind. He saw no one he knew; no one looked like him or spoke like him.

By the time the sun reached the western horizon, the warm afternoon wind had come on, and the colors of the land began to soften and come into focus. Six more Indian vehicles arrived, and lastly two cars with young whites, one with two men and a woman, the other with two men.

Just before the sun dropped from the flat earth, Gary Paul appeared outside of the Hogan. He approached each grouping of his Indian friends to inform them that the ceremony was ready to begin. He greeted the late-arriving whites and invited them inside, and then he motioned to Stewart with his eyes to enter the Hogan. Only children and two Indian women remained outside with the wind.

The Hogan was hexagonal in design, creating a roughly circular feeling once inside. In the middle of the dirt-floored structure, facing west and away from the entrance was a wood stove. Against the far wall, facing the fire was the Indian Priest seated on a blanket of earth-toned reds and grays, busy with the instruments of the ceremony and seemingly oblivious to the people who were filing in. To either side of the Priest, also seated on the blanket, were his assistants, and to his left, after the assistants, in a place of honor, was Gary Paul.

Stewart Turner entered the windowless Hogan. When his eyes adjusted to the light, he found a place to sit on the dirt floor against the wall a quarter of the way around the circle to the Priest's right, filling an empty space between an Indian man and one of the two whites who had arrived together. The Hogan, lit only by the glow of the fire and candles, was already hot, and the air was thick. Stewart could smell the years of piñon and juniper smoke in the timbers and mud and could see the austere life that had existed for generations in that house. He looked to his left where the two whites sat, but they did not return his glance. He looked across the space enclosed by the Hogan to where Gary Paul sat with his eyes closed, seemingly in a trance. After a few minutes, the Hogan was filled; all the people were inside a circle around the firebox, their backs to the wall, the Priest at the top of the circle. Stewart heard the Hogan door close, the remainder of daylight shut out. He could hear the dry wind blowing.

The native Priest began a slow chant that was soon joined by some of the other Indians and by Gary Paul. One of the Priest's assistants took up a soft drumbeat in smooth sync to the chanting. The chanting lasted only a few moments. The Priest passed a pouch of tobacco and cigarette papers to his left, instructing all present to roll a cigarette. While the tobacco was making the circle, the priest spoke in difficult English. "To our white brothers and sisters, we say welcome to this ceremony that was called by our friend and brother Gary Paul. All evil is left outside this house. Only good remains here. We smoke together, and we are as one, and no one makes us more or less than one before the sun has come back to us. The door to this house holds us together so we don't fall apart, and the door to this house is closed until the sun returns to us. The spirit of fire is with us in the box in the middle of this house, but we will free the fire when the sun returns to us. The fire is our brother, and we must show proper respect. We must not show disrespect to our brother by coming between the fire and the leaders of this ceremony. We have the spirit of medicine with us, and we must show our respect for the medicine and treat it like a brother. The medicine has the power to bring the evil out of us and cleanse us and we must not resist the power of the medicine. We must allow the medicine to make us free of evil."

When the tobacco reached Stewart, he rolled a cigarette and passed the material on. The priest spoke again when he saw that everyone had tobacco. "We smoke together. We send our smoke in the direction of the four winds. We do this together to become one for the success of the ceremony. The seal we create will not be broken until the sun returns to us. All evil must remain outside of this house."

And then the deep, resonant drum started again in the familiar and soothing heartbeat pace. The Indians began a chant that lasted a very long time. Through the floating light inside the Hogan, Stewart could see Gary Paul's lips moving with the chant, yet his eyes remained closed. Then he heard the white man next to him take up the chant in a rough, uncertain way. Stewart joined the chant, and as it continued, a stack of paper cups was passed around the circle. The liquid medicine, peyote tea, followed the cups, and after the tea came baskets of ripe peyote buttons cut up to bite-size pieces. Stewart filled his cup with the green tea and took several peyote buttons from the basket.

The peyote was brown and leathery outside, soft and ripe inside.

Stewart had consumed peyote illegally at his home in Flagstaff but here, in the presence of the Native American Church, the use was legal, and it made him feel proud to be part of the ceremony. He examined the Indian medicine, noting that little care had been taken to remove the tufts of white cotton-like strands of strychnine that was as much a part of the peyote as the boney skeleton was of a trout. He knew that the best results were achieved by slowly chewing the buttons to extract all of the medicinal juices. The strychnine would affect him; he knew that for sure, and he knew that was part of what he signed up for when he accepted Gary Paul's invitation. After drinking the tea and chewing the button, Stewart craved water, but there was no water, only more tea if he chose which he did not at that point. He glanced across the air-choked Hogan to Gary Paul, who leaned serenely against the Hogan wall, slowly chewing his peyote buttons as though they were sweet hunks of jerked venison and sipping his tea as though it was fresh spring water.

The chanting continued in apparently endless repetition. The Hogan grew hot and dim, the air thick and stagnant. One of the Priest's assistants, the fire-chief, approached the firebox from the side and fed more fuel to it. Stewart moaned within himself; he was already burning up. He thought of water to soothe his dry mouth and throat, but there was none. Before the chant was finished, the medicine made another pass around the circle. Stewart felt obliged to accept more, which he did in the smallest of portions.

When the medicine stopped making the rounds and came to a rest on the Priest's blanket of gray and red, the Priest spoke: "Gary Paul, you have called this ceremony seeking help from our heavenly Father and from your brothers and sisters here with you. Speak now of all that is in your heart and your soul and your mind. Do not be ashamed."

"Allow the medicine to work its power to help you. Speak now from your heart so that you might be free."

Stewart saw Gary Paul's eyes open, eyes that did not see any person but that looked up above the people still in a trance. He leaned forward slightly as he spoke, rocking back and forth. "Oh Heavenly Father and brothers and sisters, thank you for this opportunity to share my troubles and sorrows. I will not speak long, for there is much to say by others."

"Mmmm," was the reply from the Priest then copied by the others. "Thank you, Father, for showing me the path to the Indian way and for bringing me to my Indian brothers and sisters and for allowing me to share this beautiful ceremony."

"Mmmm," answered many of the Natives.

"I was born in a land where man fences himself in, where man fights with his neighbors out of uncontrolled fear, where man slays nature calling it progress, where man is slave to money, where man poisons his body with the food he eats and his mind with television..."

"Mmmm." Stewart watched Gary Paul. He was serene, at peace, and as composed as any person was. He looked at home. Other white guests were moaning loudly from the effect of the Peyote, failing to compose themselves to the ceremony. Across the Hogan, another of the whites spread out on the dirt floor in apparent pain. Stewart noticed that no one paid attention to the wailers except for a large Indian man seated near the door. This man wore a long black hair braid, traditional clothing and footwear, and copious amounts of silver and turquoise jewelry. His face was etched from wind and stone. His dark eyes reflected the fire as he examined each of the white moaners.

The Priest spoke, "You must let the medicine work. The medicine will release the evil from your body and mind. Do not be ashamed of the evil that is inside of you. Let the medicine cleanse you."

As if on cue, the white man next to Stewart vomited violently. The "Fire-Chief" came with a small shovel and bucket and scooped the evil from the dirt floor. Stewart also felt the need to vomit, but he fought to refrain, and he desperately fought to show respect for the ceremony that Gary Paul shared in his transformed self.

The big Indian with the dark eyes watched everything. The wailers wailed on, frequently at a pitch and with such desperation that it was difficult to hear the chant that had started up again. Stewart suppressed the vomit but prayed for a drink of cool water and a breath of fresh air.

When the chanting and the drums were silent, Gary Paul spoke again while the big Indian with cold eyes held Stewart frozen. "So thank you, Father, for bringing me to this good place from the evil place where I was born and for bringing me into your house and making me one of your people with my brothers and sisters who now sit at the same circle as me."

The Priest was leaning toward one of his assistants, conferring.

"There are some who are with us for the first time. The medicine is strong. It works strongly. For those who are new friends, we will take ten minutes and permit you to step outside."

One of the whites across from Stewart stood at once, but a loud voice, that of the big Indian, called out in the native tongue. The priest listened patiently, occasionally nodding and acknowledging with the non-committal, "Mmmm." Without understanding the Indian words, it was obvious to Stewart that the big Indian spoke in anger. When the big Indian finished, the Priest spoke, in hard English. "We welcome our fellow priest and brother who comes to us from the Lukachukai Mountains, where many of our house live and where many of our traditions and treasures are guarded so well. It is an honor to have you at our ceremony. We ask you to speak your heart and your mind in the white tongue, not only for our new friends but also for some of our own people who do not hear the old tongue as well. All should hear these matters and concerns you speak of."

The big Indian was much younger than the old priest, and he submitted to English only out of respect for age and place, but his voice contained anger. "Why do we conduct our ceremony in the tongue of the white man?" he asked in perfect, white-educated English. "On the mountain we do not do so. If some of our people do not know the tongue of the old, then they must learn if we want our language to survive. This ceremony is not an authentic ceremony in the white tongue. The medicine does not work in the way it should with white words. Why do we allow this door to be opened before the sun comes back to us? Have we forgotten that the force that holds us together is broken when the door is opened before the sun arrives? Have we forgotten that the spirit of the fire and the spirit of the medicine and the spirit of good flies out the door when it is opened to a dark world? Have we forgotten that evil waits outside that door? On the Mountain, the door would not be opened until the light of morning crawled through the cracks like a spider. A person would rather die than open the door before the sun returned to us."

"Why do we even permit these white people among us while we conduct our ceremony? On the Mountain, we would not allow it. This is a sacred ceremony. This is an Indian ceremony. The medicine is Indian medicine. The medicine will not work for white people, and it will not work for Indian people when white people are present. Why do we permit this ceremony to be defiled by strangers who crawl around the sacred floor like snakes? Why do we permit their disrespect? Can't we see what the medicine tells us? This is just another trip for white people. Don't we know that these whites, when they finish crawling around on their bellies, will try to take this away from us just as they have taken everything else? How much more can we allow to be stolen from us? Now they want our ceremony and our medicine."

The big Indian paused, then let a bit of laughter escape from his mouth. "Gary Paul is our brother. Gary Paul is an Indian, accidentally born with white skin, but that's not his fault. But open the door now."

The old Priest spoke then, "You speak well, my brother. You speak honestly and with power from your heart. But your way is not always our way. We respect and we understand your way. These whites are our guests, and we wish to treat them just as we wish to be treated when we are in their house. Only in this way can we find peace. We use the white tongue as a man would use a hammer, in the way of a tool but never to replace his hand. The medicine is strong, this you know. We open the door this one time not to let the spirits flee but to show compassion and understanding. We hope those who step out will bring a heart full of good back into this place."

On the Priest's instructions, the door was opened. The whites, except for Stewart and Gary Paul, filed past the big Indian to the outside, into the night. Stewart looked for Gary Paul's eyes, but they were hidden from view. He wished desperately to remain inside and to avoid the desecration and sacrilege the Indian from the Mountain had spoken of. But the Strychnine of the Peyote and the thick heat of the Hogan would not permit it.

Outside, in the night's dark, cool air, Stewart moved quickly away from the others into the trees. He vomited, but without the intensity, the abdominal pain would have indicated. The pain and discomfort was immediately gone. In its place came a serenity he'd never experienced before. He looked up, appreciating the silent sky, the stars, and the blue, black universe, and felt comfortable with his place in the world. He could feel the air's perfect temperature on his skin, and though the sky was clear, he could smell a rain coming from the West. As he walked back to the Hogan, he passed an Indian and a white standing together. The white man offered the Indian a synthetic drug in capsule form, but the Indian refused and said, "It is dangerous to mix the medicine with anything else except for clean water." He laughed, pointing to the wilderness surrounding the Hogan. "It's not allowed. You might go out there and never return." The white man laughed also, swallowing the capsule himself. He winked at the Indian and replied with a superior tone, "But, you see, I consider everything I take into my body as a sacrament." Stewart was embarrassed by the white man's comment but said nothing. He returned to his place in the Hogan. Gary Paul's eyes remained closed to the world. Chanting began, and as it progressed, it had a strong and mesmerizing effect on him. The Peyote medicine was passed again. Stewart accepted the same amount as he had the first time.

After the long chanting, the Priest called on any who cared to share their problems to do so. The lone white woman present, who sat quietly throughout the ceremony, broke into a loud wail and cry. Three times, she cried out: "I am a sinner among sinners. May God save my soul." Then she stopped and sobbed desperately into her hands.

"Mmmm."

The Indian man next to Stewart spoke out. "I want to pray for my daughter. I want to pray for her to get a good education so she and her children don't have to live in the crushing reservation poverty. And so that she isn't like her older brother, who drank whiskey and shot himself to death last year in the white town. I want to pray for good schools on the reservation, and I want her to find out what happened to my sister's daughter, who we can't find, but I don't want her to end up like my sister, drunk on whiskey all day living in the white man's town."

'Mmmm.'

Then a small Indian man with the wrinkled face of a man who had worked out in the sun and walked a thousand miles a year quietly spoke, "I need help for my son. My son needs surgery in the white hospital. He needs it real bad."

"Mmmm."

Stewart could hear tears from all the angels in the Hogan. A long silence was left to wear itself out. The speaking was replaced by drums and chanting.

Soon Stewart heard nothing but songs as if they came from within him and as if the soothing sound held him up. He could no longer feel his body. The medicine had released him to where the only thing that existed were his senses. With his back against the rough-hewn timber and his legs crossed, he was in perfect comfort. The light flowed placidly throughout the Hogan, tinting the walls with downy-soft blues, and reds, and greens. He released his mind, like the cutting of a taut cord, from its physical constraints. He could feel it free-floating, serene, and at peace.

When the long chant was over, the Priest spoke, "It is the time of the water ceremony. It is the time for all of us to take fresh, clean water together. Water is our brother and must be treated with respect. We must give thanks for the water we take."

A sense of joy filled Stewart. He could think of only one thing he wanted, and that was water. From a dark corner entered the water maiden carrying a shiny silver pail full of water. She came to the middle of the Hogan, near the firebox. She set the pail down so that the Native American Church symbol on the pail faced the fire.

The maiden lowered herself to the dirt floor, sitting humbly next to the water, her eyes cast down. The chanting started, but the maiden remained silent, eyes down. She was perhaps sixteen. She wore a dress of purple and maroon with high deerskin moccasins and silver buttons. Her hair was a deep, rich black, braided thick and loosely onto her back. Her skin was pure and smooth, a deep mauve and vermilion combination that seemed to have reflected onto her from the stone walls and cliffs, and so delicate that it seemed forbidden to touch, only to be admired as an honored member of the Native American Church. Her eyes were dark and hidden within the humility that her position respected. She was the purest living creation Stewart had her encountered. The Indian from the mountain watched Stewart watch the maiden.

"… Water is our brother, water is our sister, water sustains us and gives us life and must be treated with all of our respect at all times." Chanting. The maiden did not chant; she did not move. She might have been carved of stone. The deep, full colors of her clothing flowed around her. Stewart could see nothing but the maiden. He could smell the water she brought, cold and fresh.

"… Water comes to us from the sky. It blesses us and our land."

"Water runs down to us from the mountains and the canyons to replenish us. Water is the pure substance from the heavens, a gift to us. It is wrong to make clean water dirty and good water bad."

Chanting. Stewart could see the Indian maiden. He could see her in the canyons, deep within on a cool summer day, next to a deep pool of water carved from soft stone, kept fresh by a narrow stream from above. He could see her alone for countless miles except for a young Indian man. He could see them swimming in the pool, waiting for the sun to break over the cliff face above so they could lay in the sun to dry and warm themselves. He could see them on the stone, unaware of the hour, or the month, or the year, or of the existence of the white man.

"...Water sustains us; water is free. It belongs to no one. It is wrong to capture water or to hold it prisoner. Water turns the brown earth green and makes our fields of corn grow. Water waits for us in the mountains in winter and comes to us in the spring and summer in the streams and rivers. Water is life; water must be treated with respect."

Chanting. The maiden remained unmoved. Stewart could see her. He could see her past, present, and future. He could see her beauty. He wanted to speak to her, to tell her to run swiftly, back to the canyon, back to the pool of fresh water fed by the springs in the mountains. But he could not speak. He did not know how to speak to the maiden. Her youthful beauty entranced him; he could see nothing but her. Delicate color enshrouded her.

"...Treat water as a friend with great respect. We capture water in this pail for only a brief time, and then we free it by taking it into our bodies, a gift from the sky. The pail is sacred. It has the symbol of the Native American Church that is recognized by the entire American Nation. The symbol must always face the fire. When the water comes to you, treat it as a friend. Pick the pail up and pass it to your neighbor. Do not drag the pail in the dirt. Keep the symbol facing the fire. Take water from the pail and free it once again." Chanting. The maiden stood with the grace of a ballerina. Her eyes remained downcast. She moved lightly around the circle, giving each person a small cup. Stewart wanted to speak to the maiden when she came near, but she passed by silently, her colors trailing behind her, without looking at him or anyone else. He could not speak. He did not know how. He wondered if he would ever be able to speak again. As she passed by, he could smell the fresh earth. She returned to the water pail. The maiden continued around the Hogan. Stewart witnessed one of the white men drag the pail through the dirt to the person beside him. Stewart was greatly angered by the white man's disrespect to the water. He could sense the big Indian's anger. His heart told him to reprimand the white man, but his soul stopped him. It was not his place. When the maiden had delivered water to all of the people, she returned the pail to the top of the circle facing the fire and resumed her quiet sitting place. "Celebrate water."

The chanting and the drums continued for timeless lengths of time. Stewart closed his eyes and relaxed his body, allowing the sounds to penetrate him. Again, he permitted his mind to float free. He felt the universe at peace within him because everything he had control over was serene. He could sense freshness overtaking him. He became aware of a change in the drumbeat and the songs. They were faster, lighter, and happier. Though his eyes remained closed, he could feel the joy of the participants. The speed of the songs increased steadily over a long period of time. He opened his eyes to look around the circle, unable to find an unhappy face, except for the Indian from the Mountain, who betrayed no emotion of any kind. Many of the people had tears of joy on their faces.

Virgin light had begun to make its' way into the Hogan. The long night was over.

The drums and the songs stopped. The gathering quietly expressed their pleasure and happiness. The Hogan door was opened wide, allowing morning light and air to pour in. The sky was a soft gray with no direct sun. As he walked about to unwrap his body, Stewart felt a fine mist building up on his face and arms. The rain was so light that he could not feel it falling from the sky onto his skin. There was only a moistness.

Everything he saw was bright and fresh. The earth was new with a unique tone, and droplets of rain on the sage enhancing the red stone hues that surrounded their world. He walked slowly, yet with a confidence and a harmony he'd never felt before and which, he believed, would always be with him. After some time he became aware of a young Indian man walking beside him. The Indian seemed to be directing him back toward the Hogan. When Stewart smiled at the Indian, the young man said, in a kindly voice, "The medicine is powerful. If you wander too far, you might never return. You might walk into another world." Stewart returned the smile, nodded, and started back to the Hogan, mist still floating in the air.

As he waited for the Indian women to prepare the Hogan for a meal that they would all take together, Stewart listened and overheard negotiations between one of the white men and the Indian who had prayed during the ceremony for money to help his son. The white man was looking over his shoulder to where the cars and trucks were parked when he said, "My car is worth eight hundred dollars, so I should get fifteen hundred peyote buttons for it."

The Indian man grunted, "The medicine is sacred. I can't sell it like a bottle of liquor."

The white man laughed like a man who enjoyed bartering. “You told us in the Hogan that your son needed help. You need the money for him. I’ve got the car. You’ve got Peyote. You can sell the car for a lot more than you can sell the Peyote for.”

“But it’s sacred,” said the Indian with a desperate look on his face. Stewart felt frozen, still somewhat under the power of the Peyote. He stared silently at the Indian and the white man when Gary Paul suddenly was present. Gary Paul quietly approached the Indian and handed him the keys to his Volkswagen. “Sell this car, Askuwheteau,” he said. “Get your son what he needs. The medicine is not for sale.” Then he walked away.

Stewart followed Gary Paul. When he caught up with him, he said, “Gary, wait. You can ride home with me.” Gary smiled.

“No thanks, Stewart. I want to walk back.”

Stewart chuckled. “Come on, Gary. It’s forty miles.”

“I know. It will be a nice walk.” As he watched Gary Paul walk out of sight, Stewart could sense that the Big Indian had exited the Hogan and was staring at him. Stewart understood why the Big Indian would be staring at him. He understood that the Big Indian felt the need to try to protect the Navajo ceremony from non-Natives. Stewart agreed with what the Big Indian said and felt.

Stewart was glad that he was fortunate to experience the Navajo Peyote ceremony. But now he thought the Big Indian was right. As he walked toward his car, Stewart thought that he should be the last white man to experience the Navajo ceremony except, maybe, for Gary Paul. Mr. Sax and the Red Canoe: Mr. Sax is dying. He used to play the saxophone, so everyone just calls him Mr. Sax. All the rivers in southwestern Montana are at flood stage. The snowmelt of May and early June, along with cold, heavy rains, have brought the rivers up to and, in some places, over their banks, even up here in the mountains not so far from the source of the river. The lowlanders who built their homes and ranches in the floodplain downriver are complaining that the County has abandoned them.

It’s Mr. Sax’s kidneys that are the problem. Four times each day he locks himself in his room at his large log house, a short distance downriver from my cabin, to give himself his treatment, as he calls it. He complains that the treatment bloats him. He hates it.

I get up early and walk in the cold mountain rain through a tunnel of thick, dark green pines toward his house that always has smoke puffing up from his chimney. He has laid a morning fire, and maybe he's been awake all night. I don't ask him to go for coffee with me at the cafe about two miles down the road. I'm afraid I might interrupt his treatment, and I'm pretty sure he cannot walk that far anymore. He is a lot of decades older than me. He used to be a strong walker before his current condition took hold. He's an older good friend. We have done a lot of outdoor things together, mostly canoeing. I watch the river as I walk. I'm familiar with all the markers.

At any given point along the river, I can tell with a glance whether it is up or down from the day before. I stay on the far side of the river, away from the road. There can be unwanted noise disturbing my musing from passing trucks and tribes of motorcycles. I am fascinated and excited by this surge of nature. I'm eager to devote my full attention to it so that when it passes, and when it's back to its normal flow, I will be able to tell myself that I participated in the event as much as possible. I don't want to let it skip by or be uninvolved with it. In reality, the river is my neighbor. What I really want is my bronze-colored canoe to take me on the river when it's wild and aggressive or even angry.

My bronze canoe and me on the river. That's the picture I see when the river is just right. Whether I can find someone to go with me or not.

Despite his age, before he started the treatments, that person probably would have been Mr. Sax.

Before I get to the cafe, a moose crosses the river, easily keeping its nose above water. When it enters the rough water, I think this will be something to see, the moose struggling against the powerful flood. Maybe it will be swept downstream. To my surprise, the moose handles the river without a lot of drama.

I cross over on a small bridge to the cafe. The waitress passes by to pour my second cup of coffee. "The river is pretty high. Hasn't crested yet, according to the radio. They say it hasn't been this high since 1987. The commercial guys have canceled all their trips." She says all this without looking at me, while staring out the window at the rain and the river. The cafe is empty except for me and the owner, who is paying bills in the back room. They are waiting for the rain to stop and for the river to go down and for the tourists to show up. They wait like fisherman waiting for the salmon fly to hatch.

I'm happy to hear a confirmation that this flood is beyond normal, but at the same time, I'm a touch disappointed that its uniqueness only travels back about 35 years, according to the waitress. I was hoping for 100 years. A reprieve from the clouds and rain comes when I have finished my morning hike. The grass and the bush have left my boots and jeans as wet as though I'd waded knee-deep into the river. The route of my morning hike descends onto a little mud road near Mr. Sax's property. His garage door is open. He is selling off the tools and equipment that he knows, and everyone else knows, he will never use again. Rudy, who originally sold Mr. Sax's land to him, has come around to buy. Mr. Sax calls me over. "Need any tools? I'm selling them cheap. I won't need them anymore. I'd rather sell them to you than to Rudy. He's a stingy son of a bitch."

I walk around the garage. In one ear, I hear Rudy bargaining as if he was in Istanbul's central bizarre. Somehow, it doesn't seem right to me to haggle a dying man over the price of his personal possessions. I admit thinking, at the same time, that Mr. Sax will never use them again. There is a sour sound to Rudy's voice, trying to work the asking price down. It's not that Mr. Sax seems to object; he's also bargaining as if it matters.

Somehow it just seems an unnecessary insult to tell a dying man that his worldly possessions are basically worthless; that it's not much more than junk you're buying as a favor and that you're paying him anything at all only because he's an old friend and, well, because he's dying. Mr. Sax has already sold his recreational equipment. His horse is gone and all of his high-quality tack. "I'll take that maul and those two wedges," I say.

"Fifteen dollars for the lot," calls Mr. Sax. "Rudy wouldn't pay more than eight," he adds.

"Fine," I say, "and I'll take the ax and snow shovel." Mr. Sax nods and retorts as he writes in his notepad, "I've made eighty dollars so far."

"Not bad," I answer. "Need a pair of skis?"

I see he has a pair hanging in his garage. I wonder how long it has been since he skied. "No, thanks. I've got a pair that is holding up so far."

Mr. Sax makes his way, shuffling over to my corner of the garage, while Rudy examines a box of miscellaneous wrenches and screwdrivers. "Goddamn thief is robbing me," he mutters of Rudy.

Shaking my head, I look at Mr. Sax. "Come on, Sax, you've known him for years," I say. "Don't let him get under your skin. Put a sign out on the highway and get some people in here."

Mr. Sax's face shows disgust. "I don't want a bunch of goddam strangers grubbing through my stuff. I'd rather my friends steal it from me so I can complain."

"I'll oblige you," I say, laughing.

Mr. Sax laughs one better. "No, you won't, you son-of-a-bitch. You won't get my canoe. I've got other plans for it. That's your problem, so go ahead and cry."

I keep looking for what I really want. "You got any extra canoe paddles?" He has multiple pairs of paddles, the best money can buy, but it's his red ones I want.

"Yes, I do."

"Want to sell them?"

"Nope. I don't want anyone to have those but me. I might bury them right next to me."

I merely nod. I don't argue. I don't take the bait, so Mr. Sax goes on. "That's the beauty of being in my predicament. I can sell for nothing or not sell for anything. The laws of economics no longer apply to me, but when I used to race those Saskatchewan boys in the five-mile canoe sprints, then I would have paid anything for a good paddle if it would help me win."

"I understand," I say, picking up my goods and starting down the road.

Mr. Sax follows me out and down the road a few steps. "You're a lucky man," he says. Comparatively speaking, there was no denying the truth of the statement, but I couldn't just nod my assent and walk on, so I spoke stupidly on the spur of the moment, and in so doing, I basically said nothing.

"Why's that?" I ask.

"Because you get to chop firewood," says Mr. Sax with a sigh. "That's the truth, Sax. I do chop a lot of firewood. I'm an expert at chopping firewood."

Walking back to my little cabin, carrying my new maul, ax, wedges, and snow shovel, I see my bronze canoe leaning against my woodpile like a beached whale. The appearance of the sun makes me uneasy. The worst of the weather, the peak of the river, may have passed me up while I was engaged in commerce. My canoe, still laying upside-down in what may as well have been a cactus patch, irritated me. It rained hard that night, and the river came up higher, maybe even higher than earlier floods, I hoped. The morning was turbulent with a hard, overcast sky that threatened to continue with the heavy rain. Today was the day to take advantage of the challenge or to lose the opportunity altogether. Tomorrow might be too late. I would be just a spectator if I didn't take the run today.

My only excuse is that there was no one to go with me. But it was only an excuse, and I knew it. My canoe was built to be handled solo, and I'd done so countless times, though not in water with this much attitude. As soon as I was in the current of the river, I could feel that I was in trouble and that I'd never faced moving water this strong and unleashed.

The force of the river was easily the controlling factor, not me or my paddle strokes or my experience. But I was in the middle of the current, keeping the canoe in line with the flow of the water, not getting the canoe crosswise with the flow, and knowing that now I had to ride it out, if possible.

I didn't know what Mr. Sax was originally doing that morning, but when I rounded the bend and first saw him, he was standing down by the river in back of his house with one of his expensive red canoe paddles in his hand. He looked upriver and saw me just as I was listing starboard, digging my paddle in to correct my angle to the river, when I was slammed by a rogue wave that pushed me crosswise and then a second wave that flipped the canoe toward a bad sweeper. When I surfaced, I was out of the canoe and choking on swallowed river water. I was being carried downstream at a torrid pace. My paddles were gone, and my canoe was a few feet away from me upside down.

Swimming furiously, I was able to get ahold of the canoe, hoping I could guide it to the bank near where Mr. Sax was standing. Then I felt the cold water for the first time along with the bruises on my legs and the lack of strength in my arms. Ahead of me was a section of genuine rapids, and I was nearly in the middle of the river again. Trying to save the canoe suddenly seemed foolish. I had to save myself. I was embarrassed under Mr. Sax's eyes, but I abandoned the boat to swim for the shore.

When I left the boat to begin making my way toward the bank, I went under momentarily, taking another full measure of water before my life jacket brought me to the surface. The swift rising and falling of the floodwater swept into my nose and mouth as my lower body slammed into submerged rocks and tree branches. The enemy, I thought, was the weakness in my legs and arms. My energy was leaking out fast. I recall two thoughts in succession. The first was whether I was going to make the riverbank, and the second was wondering what the hell Mr. Sax was shouting angrily about.

Somehow, I was able to reach the riverbank where Mr. Sax was standing. There was nothing left in me. But Mr. Sax started slapping me with his red paddle, his eyes full of tears, screaming, "Drown, you fool, you goddamn no-good fool, drown." He was actually trying to beat me back into the river.

I could not figure it out, but I was so close to being physically finished that my mind quit trying. I remember thinking the morbid thought that Mr.

Sax was nearer to death than I was, so I should still have enough strength to reach up and pull the paddle from his hands, which I did. I threw the damn thing into the river to stop the beating. Mr. Sax just kept on screaming at me.

When I was able to pull myself up, I stood on the bank, dripping wet, cold to the bone, staring at Mr. Sax, who was continuing to attack me with everything he had. I was not going to bother chasing the unmanned canoe. I didn't want it anymore. I had failed. For all I cared it could float down that wild river until it reached the placid water at Fort Peck Reservoir behind the damn dam hundreds of miles downriver.

I had to disarm Mr. Sax from swinging his second canoe paddle at me. He was insane with a fury beyond belief. I retaliated by deflecting his effort to knock me back into the river with his other red paddle. I was yelling at him with more anger than I knew I possessed. "What the hell are you doing, you crazy old man. Quit hitting me with that paddle, or I'll throw you in the river."

"Then throw me into the river," he yelled back with an equal amount of anger, still swinging the paddle at me. "That would be better than dying the way I'm dying. Why didn't you give me the opportunity to canoe the river with you? You dumb bastard. Instead, you came canoeing down this river like it was a Sunday afternoon, right by my house to be sure I saw you, just to taunt me. Were you trying to show me that you could do it, which you obviously can't, you weak piece of crap? Your way of telling me that I couldn't even try it because I was dying will be eternally resented."

I was absolutely stunned but still furious. "You stupid-son-of-a-bitch, Sax. I couldn't take you into that river. You're not well. You're less than not well. It would have been murder, you dumbass."

Mr. Sax did not lower his voice or his fury. "I'm not well, you say?"

"That's one way to put it. It would have been murder, you say? Well, that's all my choice, asshole, not yours. There are worse things than murder, you idiot. First, you sneak by my house to go for coffee, trying to avoid me, and now you try to run this river in a canoe at flood stage, knowing I would see you, just to show off. What is it? Are you afraid you'll catch my condition by being near me?"

I truly could not believe what Mr. Sax was saying, but neither could I doubt that he actually meant what he was saying. I calmed down a bit and said, "Sax, I'm sorry, I really am, but don't be crazy. I couldn't, and I wouldn't in a thousand years have thought of taking you into that river. It was just too dangerous. It damn near killed me."

Mr. Sax turned fully calm. He just stared at me for maybe a full moment before speaking, not yelling. "Did it ever occur to the idiot you are that I might decide, that I might prefer, to go out canoeing a flooding river rather than by going out the way I am? That I might choose to have my obituary announce that I died trying to run a wild river in flood stage in a canoe instead of that I died at home after a long illness. Shit, come on." There was a very long pause because I was speechless, and Mr. Sax was not going to let me off the hook. Finally, I said, "No, Sax, that did not occur to me. I did not think of that. I did not."

Mr. Sax sort of smiled. "Of course you didn't, of course. Just remember, I loved every outing we did together, and I would have loved this one."

Again, I paused before any words came to me. Finally, I said, "I'm sorry, Sax. I certainly did not think of that. I loved the time we spent together in the wild too. But right now, I'm freezing and numb from my toenails to my forehead. I'll see you soon. I'm going to my cabin to warm up."

As I was walking away, I remembered my grandmother saying, when I was young, that when you get smacked, it's usually for a good reason. I hope this was somehow for a good reason. I'd been smacked by the river, and I'd been smacked by Sax this day. As I was walking stiffly down my pothole-filled road, I heard Mr. Sax call out, "My red canoe and paddles are yours, but not until I'm gone." The Shadow of the Trap, Arthur and Stewart were up before the others. They stood at the edge of the canyon, peering into its vastness.

"This is still the main gorge," said Arthur.

"It's immense," said Stewart.

"A man could wonder lost forever in the main gorge, say nothing of the side canyons and beyond."

"Or he could simply lose himself."

"And be swallowed up by the earth."

On the rim, in the high country, the wind was still cold. In early May at 7,500 feet elevation, a lingering winter was as probable as an early spring. The night before had been windy and cold. The five men arrived late and slept on the rim. Now the first light was in the sky. Arthur gathered wood, and Stewart started the fire. Against the morning, chill a large, crackling fire was built. Arthur set a fry pan into the flames without waiting for coals to develop. He steadied the pan on burning logs. Stewart tossed a thick piece of meat with a fine rind of fat into the fry pan. Two of the others, Jim and Kurt, woke to the fire exuding its warmth. The last of the party, Martin, remained curled in his sleeping bag.

"It's cold," said Kurt, shivering. His body was wrinkled.

"It's the wind that makes it really cold," said Jim. He stood near the fire, very still, his hands in his pockets.

"The hike will warm you up soon enough," said Stewart. "We've cut three miles off by coming this way," said Arthur.

"Will it still take us six hours?" asked Jim.

"Five," answered Stewart. "But when you're done, you'll be glad it was three miles less."

Of the group, only Arthur and Stewart had previously hiked the canyon's trails. Deliberately they had not informed the others of the difficulty of the hike, certain if they did, none would come. Arthur had expressed the hope that at least one or two would be grateful. Stewart scoffed at the notion. Arthur wanted three to see the wonders at the bottom of the canyon.

Stewart wanted them to see how difficult the hike was.

It was Arthur who was infatuated with the canyon—and with all of the wilderness. He approached his trips away from civilization with the belief that he could gain a sense of universal and perfect order from the wild by solitary observation. He once said, after ten days alone in the desert, that evil did not exist in the wilds. It was Arthur's belief that he could gather its truth and its secret. He believed he could conquer the barrier between man and nature and blend them again if only he could see enough and understand enough. If Arthur could have changed himself to a tree, he probably would have done so.

Stewart would have never settled for being a tree, not any kind of a tree, not even a redwood. He wanted to be seen as outstanding, to be noted and acclaimed for endeavor (never mind which endeavor, for it did not matter to

Stewart). His wish was to be recognized as unique among men (of those proclaimed daily in the outdoor magazines and films) and to avoid being known as mediocre in what he'd been convinced was a dull, mundane world. But Stewart was an honest person, and he could not say that he had achieved competence or excellence in any sphere. He had never been the first or the best at anything. His work was as a bureaucrat. He could not invent, fix, or even operate machinery, nor could he run faster or farther than other men. He could not play his trumpet by ear or by written music, and women were not drawn to him as moths are drawn to a flame. His family did not have a prominent name, and he had no children—no vicarious hope.

So Stewart, believing that true competence had eluded him in his life (since he was thirty-three and not started on an endeavor and since he knew true excellence came only to those who were gifted and who started very young and who achieved discipline and who never wavered), had come to believe that the rest of his life would be one of mediocrity.

Because of this, Stewart had decided to take his life while in the vast silence of the canyon and to make it appear to be an accident. This was one thing he could do. It was better to end life in that way rather than in old age after a mundane life. Then, at least, those who considered his life and death would consider it with an air of mystery and adventure and tragedy. They would discuss him. Far better, he believed, than a full life of putrid decades of rotting mediocrity. It was one way, Stewart was sure, to come into balance with nature. Contrary to Arthur, Stewart believed that man had become irretrievably broken with nature, so much so that they would fight each other until one was absolutely dominant. To Stewart's mind, only man's birth and his death were in accord with nature.

Martin crawled from his sleeping bag and struggled to the fire when Stewart and Arthur were finishing the meat they had cooked. They would be ready to begin the hike in a matter of minutes, but it was clear that Martin would not. The contents of his pack lay spread over the ground in complete chaos. Kurt and Jim, eating their breakfast by the fire, laughed at Martin's sluggish appearance. Martin was a drinker. Each night he drank, and each morning was delayed because of it.

"I'm off in ten minutes," announced Arthur.

"You'll need to stay with us in order to find your way," said Stewart.

Thick, rich clouds were grouped over the canyon. It was cold. Stewart and Arthur started out before the fire had died down and before the other three were prepared. Kurt and Jim hurried to begin, but Martin paid no mind.

Immediately on the trail, there was a steep incline of seventy feet. The packs were at fifty pounds. Each man (in accord with Arthur's instructions) carried one gallon of water. There were eleven miles to go. The exertion replaced the heat the fire had given them before.

They walked west along the rim. Pine, juniper, and oak came to the rim of the canyon. There the trees ceased absolutely, as did the flat, easy earth. The canyon, to their left and visible, was a shock to the sight. At one spot, they could see the river at the bottom of the canyon, green in color. Across and level to the eye was the canyon's southern rim, covered with green forest.

The inner canyon was red and pink, vermilion and brown, purple and yellow, gray and rust. The interior of the canyon, a slice of the earth exposed, hinted at a grand design, overwhelming to comprehend.

They reached the trailhead and began their descent. The canyon had been cut in levels, each level a sheer face of earth's time, each separated by a talus slope leading to an earlier, darker, and more somber face made permanent in stone. The trail dealt with the sheer vertical walls of up to a thousand feet by locating obscure passages where the faces had faulted and been broken down by time and then by proceeding angularly with switchbacks.

"Martin will slow us," said Arthur, leading. Stewart shrugged. "Only if we let him." "We can't leave him on his own."

"He'll be alright," said Stewart. The two leaders stopped and looked up from where they had come. Soon they saw Martin at the trailhead, beginning casually, already twenty minutes behind.

"We'll have to keep an eye on him," said Arthur. "I suppose. I wish he wouldn't have come."

"I know, but how could I say no? I couldn't tell him there wasn't enough room in the canyon."

Stewart didn't laugh. "You could have said we didn't want him to come." "No, you could have. I couldn't. . . What about Kurt and Jim?"

"They stop when we stop… like shadows. Where do you want to camp tonight?"

"At the confluence of Blue Creek and Wolf Creek."

"Fine."

“I’m anxious to get there,” said Arthur. “When I get in here, I never want to come out again.”

Stewart looked ahead to what lay before them: miles of trail leading down thousands of feet to the bowels of the earth. He was laughing to himself at his thought: He was hiking as near to the center of the earth as he could. If there was a hell, he thought, he was getting himself as close as possible. Of course, he did not believe in a hell; nor a heaven. There was nothing, as far as he could tell, nothing beyond incredible chance and unbelievable coincidence. Still he was able to laugh, going under the rim from which he had resolved not to return, considering hell in his mind, since he was unable to seriously contemplate his own death.

Arthur also considered the canyon. Here order and the forces of nature were exposed. Here was the world’s marvelous plan for any seeker to examine. He tried to imagine the geography millions of years previous when the river and the wind and the storms of moisture and sand were just beginning their work on a flat and gentle land.

He viewed a massive cube of stone, nearly square and weighing tons on tons, resting at the top of the talus slope. He could spot the place in the wall above where it fit like a piece of a puzzle and from where it had been dismembered perhaps centuries before. In his mind, he compared the block of solid stone to the blocks and bricks of man, and he laughed. He heard Stewart laughing, and he turned to him. “Are you laughing at the same thing I am?” he asked.

“No doubt,” answered Stewart.

By mid-morning the sun had disappeared behind a layer of clouds.

There was no shade on the trail, and under the heavy packs, the hikers grew hot. “This is how I like it!” shouted Arthur from twenty steps ahead. “A good test for man’s substance.”

“What of his essence?” called Stewart.

“It’s in his substance.”

“We disagree.”

“We do.”

The heat forced their sweat. At two-mile intervals, the two leaders stopped in the shade of an angled boulder to wait for the others. Both slightly resented the stops; Arthur because they detracted from the severity of the test. Frequent or even infrequent stops minimized the accomplishment, the victory. Stewart’s resentment was directed at the three they waited for. He didn't mind a stop in the shade for a rest or the fact that the intensity of the hike was lessened; he objected to doing so for the reason of the other's inability to keep up and their need to be concerned for.

As soon as Martin would reach the rest spot, Stewart and Arthur would be off again. The trail was steep, embedded with, rock and coated with a chalky dust that hung about the dry air when stirred up. Their packs pulled them down the trail, and for long stretches, they jammed their toes into the toe of their boots in the effort to hold their weight back.

In the afternoon, they came to the edge of the canyon level overlooking the first water, Wolf Creek. Wolf Creek originated in the high country and percolated down through the rock to emerge from a cave on the face of a cliff. Looking not unlike man's fountains and gargoyles, spitting a stream of water, Wolf Creek spilled out and ran down the flat stone wall to the ground below and then raced white for a half-mile to where it joined Blue Creek. In its path was spread a hundred-foot-wide swath of rich green plant and tree life standing in vivid contrast to the dominant red and brown earth and walls. Stewart paused at the rim to gaze down on precious Wolf Creek, but Arthur pushed on, faster and harder than before, sweat falling like rain from his brow, a look of sensual pleasure filling his face.

Below…Stewart found Arthur on a shaded rock within the trees surrounding Wolf Creek. His boots were off and he was drinking from the cold, foaming water. The rock he sat on was cold and felt good against hot, tired skin. Stewart selected an adjoining rock and removed his boots and drank the creek's waters. When, after more than an hour, Kurt and Jim arrived, Arthur and Stewart had moved downstream to where the two creeks met. There they set up a camp. Another forty minutes passed before the arrival of Martin. There was pain in the faces of the three.

"I had no idea it would be like that," Martin said. He acted as if he'd been betrayed.

"I didn't either," said Kurt.

Jim nodded in agreement. "It was a son-of-a-bitch. I wouldn't have come if I'd known."

Stewart and Arthur, with different attitudes and longer to recover, listened patiently. They did not speak or sympathize. Martin spoke again in a still resentful, complaining voice. "We still have to climb out; I'll never make it."

"Going out is no more difficult than coming in," said Arthur in an effort to assuage the three. "In fact, it's easier."

"Like hell!" said Martin, his anger flaring at Arthur.

"That just can't be," agreed Kurt. Stewart took some pleasure in the conversation of complaint. If he died within the canyon, he would not hike out with the others, and he knew that those who now complained would, after getting over the shock of his death, resent him for not having to make the arduous climb out of the canyon. That's how petty they were, he thought; petty might indicate incompetence. At least no one would ever think of him as petty, he thought…at least that.

Arthur, too, could not help but smile some as he watched and listened to the three. He considered the irony that their preoccupation with the work required would prevent any of them from receiving the benefit of where they were. But he did not know how to tell them, as he believed, that this was the way the world worked and that they should submit to its truth and gain from it rather than being martyred by it. Martyrs were such a waste, he thought.

So they sat together in the cool shade by the creek, relaxed and refreshed, listening to the anguish of the three who were somewhere they had not knowingly or consciously asked to be, who did not know what to do with themselves while they were there, and who dreaded the thought of leaving…

II

In the morning, before sunrise, Stewart was awakened by Arthur's whisperings. The air was chilled and fresh, almost cold, and Stewart could hear the creek running.

"Stewart…wake up. Stewart…"

"I'm awake."

"Let's go fishing…and trapping."

"Trapping?"

"We'll give it a try." Arthur was sitting up in his sleeping bag, grinning. His long hair was tangled and matted. The three were asleep, enveloped within their bags. Next to Martin on a stone was a half-consumed bottle of liquor.

"Alright," said Stewart. "But keep it quiet. I don't want to wake these guys up…we'll just have to wait for them if we do."

"They wouldn't come anyway…it's too early for them. We'll bring their breakfast back."

Both men dressed quietly and quickly. From their packs, they took the tackle and gear that would be needed and started downstream along the Blue. The sand path along the creek was stained dark from the morning's dew.

"These long mornings should provide some good fishing," said Arthur. "I want to set up a trap too, before the creatures get scarce for the day." "What kind of trap?"

"Primitive," laughed Arthur.

"And what are you trapping for?"

"Anything that has the misfortune to get trapped."

Beyond primitive, Arthur's trap was crude and simple. On a flat slab stone, he propped up a twenty-pound rock with a stick. Triple strands of #8 fishing line were tied to the stick, and a hunk of cheese as bait was set under the tilted rock. Arthur placed himself sixty feet away among gray boulders and against a small cottonwood tree. He waited patiently with his eyes never leaving the uplifted rock, and when he spoke, it was in a hushed whisper. Stewart waited for a time but then grew impatient and walked down to the creek. He was always waiting, he thought, to see the result of someone else's endeavors. He started to fish.

For an hour, Stewart heard nothing from Arthur. Then pebbles hitting the rocks near him caught his attention. He saw Arthur motioning him over. He left his fishing pole and circled slowly in order to come up behind Arthur with as little disturbing movement or sound as possible. When he was at Arthur's shoulder, Arthur pointed to the rock but did not speak. Cautiously approaching the trap was a small rodent. Stewart watched for a minute until Arthur turned to look at him as if to say, 'Now look at this.' He pointed again, but this time off to the side, eight feet from the trap. There, stealthily waiting and hiding, was a rattlesnake whose intent was fixed on the rodent more even that was the trappers.' The rodent was wary in its approach to the bait. The snake did not move until the rodent had come to a position which placed the uplifted stone between the two creatures. Then came the snake, leading with a probing tongue and coiling near the trap stone. It struck with such speed that Arthur and Stewart were caught, surprised, and left uncertain of whether the snake had made a hit. But almost immediately the venom began to paralyze the rodent and then, within the shadow of the trap, to kill it. The snake slid in to claim its prey. Arthur jerked the fish line; the stick fell out, and the stone came down on the snake, not killing it but trapping it firmly at a point where the trap stone and ground stone made a near-complete snake jail.

"Oh!" started Stewart, surprised by the action that came swiftly and certainly.

"Got him!" cried Arthur. "Jesus, you did."

"This is better than I'd hoped for."

"A snake?" asked Stewart. "We can eat him…and have a beautiful hat band."

"He's not dead yet."

"We'll take care of that."

When they reached the stone that lay on the writhing snake, the snake was trying to strike and kill itself. Arthur said: "This is excellent…he hasn't bit himself yet. We can kill him without mutilating the skin…isn't the skin beautiful?

"How will you kill him?" asked Stewart.

Arthur examined the position of the snake under the stone to judge where the head lay. At that point, he stepped up on the stone and stepped down with his weight. Blood squirted out from under the rock. Stewart looked away. Arthur laughed at him. The snake ceased its writhing. While they fished, Arthur wore his dead snake around his neck. When they returned to camp, the other three were sitting around the fire.

"Where the hell have you two been?" asked Kurt. "You were gone when we woke."

"What do you have there?" Jim asked Arthur.

"Breakfast," said Arthur with a wide grin. "Fish and snake." He tossed the fish and the snake to the center of the three, next to the fire. "Cook 'em up."

Stewart could see that Arthur enjoyed the act. The three cooked the fish but all declined to handle the snake. Stewart, too, enjoyed the scene, having come in with Arthur from the hunt, coming onto the three woman-like camp-fire dwellers; coming in with game to cook for the group's morning meal. Stewart felt good that day. It was clear that the three were impressed by Arthur and Stewart's ability to provide sustenance from the land. No doubt, he thought, they believed such things only occurred in fiction or history. They sat around the fire after consuming the fish, eating chocolate and raisins, and drinking black, boiled coffee. Stewart and Arthur related the story of the snake's demise, and Arthur acted out the part of the snake, and they all laughed. Arthur worked on skinning the snake as they talked. Stewart had more hot coffee. He felt good that day. He felt that it was not the day to take his life.

Arthur spent the second day alone; Stewart did also. Arthur hiked downstream toward the river beyond where he and Stewart had ventured the day before. He started early, taking his fishing pole and a lunch. Along the walls enclosing the side canyon, Arthur searched with his eyes for Indian cliff-dwellings. It wasn't until he'd gone two miles that he saw a shaded opening in the wall. He climbed up, two hundred feet above the creek, to find a minor dwelling thoroughly explored and exploited by those previous to him. A decayed and cracked support beam in the opening was the only certain proof of its identity as a primitive dwelling. One minor, isolated dwelling where but a few had lived centuries before, he thought.

One dwelling where everything beyond the rim, including the knowledge that existed there, was foreign and unknown. The canyon walls were the same as then, so was the river; it could be the same for a man who chose to live within the walls now. He would be under her immutable laws. And then, as he walked on the dusty, rough trail, clad only in leather boots and heavy cotton pants, he felt a part of everything and that everything was a part of him. He felt that he was free of the bonds of man…

The river was cold, dark green. Arthur knew the condition of the river was a consequence of the dam that held and controlled the river over a hundred miles back. He cursed the dam for stealing the river from its naturally turbulent and muddy existence; he decried the end of awesome floods that once ripped the canyon from one end to the other. And even the times of drought when there wasn't sufficient water to cover the rugged, boulder-strewn course of the river were a tragic loss to Arthur's mind. For now, the river was controlled by poured cement and penstocks, spillways, and turbines. Yet he felt assured it would not always be so. The lake behind the dam would fill with silt one day, and then the river would break free from its barrier.

Man couldn't hold nature back indefinitely, he thought. So Arthur felt calm as he fished the cold, clear waters of the river.

Stewart took the opposite direction from Arthur, upstream along the Blue. He hadn't slept well due to a stone under his bag that he failed to find when he cleared a spot for himself. Like so many other times, he woke that morning absent a trace of the serenity that had filled him the day before.

Where was the substance that sustained life for more than hours at a time? Where was the line to tie days and events together? He walked upstream alone. At first, the creek was narrow and steep, forcing him to ford it frequently. He resented getting his boots wet. Within half a mile, the creek bed opened up and flattened. The water diminished and was eventually reduced to a trickle above ground. Stewart walked on grapefruit-sized rocks. He felt uncoordinated as he walked; his feet slipped, he had no balance, and he twisted his ankle once. He could remember in his youth being able to glide over surfaces similar to the one he was now on like a bird: graceful and sure and native. He shook his head without humor, bemoaning the decline of agility, the loss of youth, and the onset of a decay that could only culminate in an old and aged death. He thought it cruel and unjust that it began so early, before even thirty-five. Where there once had been strength was now an absence of strength—if not weakness.

Stewart came to a side canyon called Owl Canyon, which paralleled Wolf Creek Canyon. He turned north, finding that it was a shallow and narrow canyon. Soon the canyon boxed. A 150' vertical wall brought an abrupt end to

Owl Canyon's depth. Stewart walked to the monolithic wall and placed his hand against it. The wall was as smooth as poured cement. It was warm from absorbing the heat of the sun. Stewart looked straight up the face.

To Stewart's left was a narrow rockslide which had come down from one of Owl Canyon's walls. By climbing the chute, he was able to reach the point where a ledge a few feet wide was indented on the wall. Beyond the ledge, the wall soared up hundreds more feet. Stewart could look down into Owl Canyon. Smooth, straight walls reaching to the sky surrounded him on three sides. Directly below was a circular area in the shape of a bowl dug out by the sporadic waterfalls that came with the heavy rains and runoffs. The inner bowl was a rich mud. There were delicate tracks of small animals criss-crossing the smooth black surface of the receptacle bowl.

This would be the place; he felt, the place for him to die. It came to him all at once that the spot was the right one. He could leap from the ledge to the pit below. The height would be sufficient to bring him to death. There was something inviting about the dark, thick mud below; his fall would be absorbed by it, though not enough to save him, only enough so that the fear of pain would be at its lowest. And it would be quick, a matter of seconds. And final. Perhaps those who found him would conclude that he had fallen while attempting a free climb of the face. Perhaps those who discussed him would say, 'Sad, but a fine way to go, while engaged in life's adventures. A swift end without time for contemplation is the way… sure, sure.

Stewart did not remain long in the depths of Owl Canyon. Tomorrow would be the day. He did not wish to linger at this site, for if he lingered, he would think, and if thought he might become afraid to fulfill his resolution. That, he thought, would be the worst thing that could happen.

At camp Arthur's trouts from the river were cooked over an excellent set of coals, which Martin had been nurturing all afternoon. "Those are fine trout you have, Arthur," said Martin, feeling good himself having had an extra drink before the meal. "Thanks," said Arthur. "That's a fine fire you have." Jim, setting a book aside, said: "I read that it's against regulations to have an open fire below the rim."

"So?" said Stewart.

"So nothing…I'm just telling you what I read."

"But when are you going to tell us what you think?"

“I’m not thinking anything…I don’t know anything about it. I’m just telling you what the book says.”

Stewart nodded. He would say no more. Perhaps, he thought, they would remember what hc had said.

Arthur had been watching Stewart. “Well, tonight at least, we need a fire to cook these gourmet fish.”

“Sure…that’s fine,” said Jim. “I was just…”

Martin interrupted Jim. “Is this our gourmet meal?”

“Dam right,” answered Kurt.

“Then we’ll need some wine to go with it, won’t we?” said Martin. He smiled and lifted a bottle from his pack. “You son-of-a-bitch, Martin.” Laughed Arthur. “Are you sharing it?”

“But of course.”

“Is it red?” asked Jim. “But of course.”

Stewart ate the tender fish and drank the mellow wine, and though he said very little, he thought it an excellent meal, a last meal, as fine as he had ever had. He crawled into his sleeping bag when the rest did, though he was sure he wouldn’t sleep. The sky was moonless and bursting with an infinity of stars. There was a terrible silence. Stewart lay within the silence, not thinking of the day to come, watching the stars. Before the Big Dipper had moved the narrow width of the canyon, Stewart was fully asleep…

III

When Stewart woke, Arthur was gone from the camp, and Martin was up, poking at the fire. This was wrong, he thought, all wrong. This was not as it was supposed to be. He should have awakened before any of them and slid away. Better yet, he shouldn't have slept. Then they wouldn't have known when he left, that he'd slept; which direction he'd gone. For sure, it was a bad start, but then the sky was heavily overcast, and at least that was right for this day.

"How did you sleep?" called Martin to him.

"Not well—I didn't sleep until first light."

"You should've brought drink…that usually helps."

"Yes, next time I will."

"Do you want breakfast?"

"No, I'm not hungry…Where did Arthur go?"

Martin shrugged and smiled as if the answer was obvious. Stewart nodded. He dressed and sat on a rock with Martin for a cup of coffee to warm himself before he departed. "Why don't you come exploring with me?" asked Stewart, certain Martin would decline.

"No…my feet are sore from the hike in. I'm going to take it easy. We still have to climb out."

"Yes…"

As he walked from the campsite, Stewart thought he'd done the best he could to correct a bad beginning. Martin would recall what was said between them. He'd recall everything; he'd feel important and somehow closer to eternity than other men because he'd been the last to see or talk with Stewart. Martin would openly lament that he hadn't gone with him—perhaps, he would say, this wouldn't have happened had he gone along. It was all a part of the romance of death, thought Stewart. Martin would remember for others that Stewart had had a troubled night's sleep, and they would all speculate on what part that played in the tragedy. Martin would remember Stewart's lack of appetite. Most of all he would remember that Stewart had set off to do some exploring; exploring indeed, he would muse when he told the story over and over again.

When Stewart arrived at the end of Owl Canyon, he stopped to examine the pit of mud.

Its diameter was roughly twenty feet and its depth about fifteen feet. The walls of the bowl, an inverted volcano, were surprisingly steep. The mud was smooth and shiny and appeared to have only recently swallowed the last of its water. The stonewall before him, viewed from below, was as vertical as he remembered. And it did look possible, though difficult, to climb, so no one would question that he'd been climbing at the time of the fall. The chute of rocks was so simple to climb that he was almost embarrassed with himself for using it to reach his alter of death. But, he rationalized; he was engaged with matters of greater importance, which way to take in order to arrive at the same place in the end.

Stewart sat cross-legged on the stone ledge. The sky was gray, thick with clouds, and there was a dampness in the wind that blew his hair about and chilled the skin on his face. He considered which way he should leap. Certainly to take the leap face-first was the more dignified, something akin to facing the firing squad without the black hood. But then one who fell while climbing would naturally fall back first. Also, it might be easier to simply stand and take the leap if he did not have to look at what awaited him. Just stand, turn back-first, and leap before the mind or the eyes could stop him. No need to lead face-first, especially with the possibility that cynics might then debate whether he had fallen or jumped.

Stewart expected rain and wondered if his life would be over before the rain began. He peered over the side to the mud bowl that waited patiently for him. The distance up made Stewart's knees weak and his mouth dry. It made him dizzy; it always had. Acrophobia had been with him since a young age, so much so that by merely imagining a height, even while sitting in a chair, he would grow dizzy. He once believed, when he believed in such things, that he must have accidentally fallen to his death in a previous life.

His fear and his dizziness made him angry. He looked out at the day. There was nothing unusual or extraordinary about this day. It was bland and colorless. There was a mean little wind blowing. It was cold and impersonal.

Stewart thought it was not supposed to be that way, not on the day a man chose to die. He felt cheated, but he did not know how he'd been cheated. He wondered: Where was that which he had read and heard about? Where was the vision of one's life, that which appears just before death? And where was the light that was supposed to lead him into the next world? Was he not close enough to death? Was he not deserving of the comfort of the vision and that light finally provided? Stewart saw no light; he saw no vision of his life. Anger began to well in him, but it was not the dying light or the substance of the vision that inspired Stewart's rage; it was, after all, that there was no light at all, that there was no vision. These thoughts, coupled with the day's lack of uniqueness and his hearty dose of acrophobia, left Stewart angry enough to cry. He was beating his hands into stone, prepared to release a flood of emotion, when he heard a voice calling to him from below.

"Stewart? What the hell are you doing up there?"

Stewart looked down, shocked. He did not reply. How long had Arthur been there, watching and listening? He felt that he'd been screaming his thoughts and feelings and that Arthur had heard each and every one.

"Did you climb this?" asked Arthur after a minute. He looked admiringly at the vertical wall separating himself from Stewart. His expression was of respect for Stewart's climb and pleasure at the challenge it presented him. Stewart merely nodded. Arthur examined the wall, then looked over to the chute of rocks.

"You must have climbed it—that would be too easy," he said, indicating the rock chute. "It wouldn't be exciting." Stewart nodded again, but still he did not speak. It had all happened so fast and was so unexpected.

"Well, stay put…I'm coming up," called Arthur. He began to scale the wall, searching out each hand and foothold. He was grinning, and the rattlesnake skin tied around his neck below in the wind like a scarf.

Stewart sat close to the edge so he could watch Arthur climb. The process was slower than he'd thought it would be. Near halfway Arthur was unable to find the next foothold. He moved laterally across the face, searching the wall for routes as he went. He looked up and smiled. He began again when he'd found his route. He moved quickly now, as if he'd located a way with which he was somehow familiar. He was climbing with great confidence and agility when, at seventy feet from the top, the rock he grasped with his right hand broke loose, crumbling in his fingers. There was an instant when everything stood still and was silent until Arthur's foothold gave out under the additional weight and he started to fall. At some point Arthur hit an outcrop, and he was thrust out, away from the face, falling free. He landed on his back in the center of the pit with a terrible, deathly thud. One thick ring of mud waved to the edge of the bowl and then returned to the center, slowly engulfing half of Arthur's body in the black muck. Stewart witnessed Arthur's body try to bounce after impact, but the mud held him firmly like a predator. Arthur's face looked straight up.

"Arthur…" whispered Stewart. "Arthur? Are you alright, Arthur?" Arthur, lying in the center of the pit, part of his body submerged in the mud, opened his eyes after a minute; they were glassy and disoriented.

"Arthur, are you alright? Jesus, Arthur…"

"Oh God, Stewart…Oh my God." Arthur's voice was weak and disconnected. He spoke only while exhaling. "Are you alright, Arthur?"

"Oh God, I'm hurt bad…but it doesn't hurt Stewart; that's what scares me… I can't feel it."

"Where are you hurt? Can you tell?"

"My back… I think it's broken. My legs and arms, I don't know."

"Can you move?"

Arthur failed to answer. Stewart watched and waited for him to try to move, but there was no movement. "Can you move?" Stewart asked again in a dry and unsteady voice.

"I don't think so. I can't feel too much."

"I'll get you out of there, and then we'll see what's the matter." Stewart stepped into the mud and immediately sunk to his thighs. A look of horror crossed Arthur's face as the mud, displaced by the movement, started sucking at him from the center of the pit. Arthur's voice was in panic. "Get out! Get out…You'll pull me down! I'll drown in this mud…God, don't come near it!"

After a minute, the mud settled and quieted. Stewart watched Arthur's chest heave with heavy, terrified breathing. Finally, some color filtered to his face, and his breath returned to normal.

"I'll hand you a branch to pull you out," said Stewart.

Arthur became frustrated. "No, I think my arms are broken. I can't grasp anything. I'm helpless."

"I'll go for the others," said Stewart after a minute.

But Arthur cried out again. “I’m hurt bad, Stewart, do you understand? I don’t trust them—they can’t help.”

“What do you want me to do, Arthur?”

“Go for help…I need help. You’re the only one who could hike out of here fast enough to save me.”

“Go now; go by yourself. Just get to the top and walk the rim until you get to the truck or until you run into somebody. It would add two hours to go back to camp.”

“Alright, Arthur. I’ll be back as soon as possible. Hold on.” Stewart stared for a minute at the helpless Arthur, and then he started away. Arthur called him back. “Stewart, listen. I don’t want to die here; not now, not like this… God, not like this. Please, Stewart, get help.”

At the mouth of Owl Canyon was a route, too little used to be called a trail, which led through the various levels and walls and faces of the inner canyon. The route would be Stewart’s primary hope of finding his way through the maze of otherwise impenetrable geography. He found carins at the route’s beginning; where a break appeared in the first wall. The climb took Stewart five hundred vertical feet and little horizontal distance and an hour in time. He could not see Arthur. Another carin at the top of the first wall showed that he’d come the right way and pointed him north along a one-quarter-mile-wide talus slope. To his left was the great canyon’s second wall, reaching up another five hundred feet or more. In this wall, Stewart could see no break that would give him passage. He was forced to walk north along the talus slope with Owl Canyon sharp and deep to his right and an unbroken wall of red to his left. Then the rain began.

The rain came from the west. From the day’s first light, the sky had been covered gray and the air moist, yet Stewart had forgotten about the threat of rain. Now, as it began, he cursed himself for what he saw as carelessness, though he could think of nothing he would have done differently if he’d known the rain would come; he still cursed himself for not considering it. The rain did not come hard; rather, it came in a cold and quiet mist that washed everything in gray.

The hiking was difficult. There was no trail to follow, only the vague route of instinct, infrequently confirmed by silent carins. The topography was deceiving. From above, looking into the canyon, the talus slope had appeared to be a flat, gently sloping corridor between two major walls. In fact, Stewart found the slope was anything but flat and gentle. At regular intervals, there were dry runoff ravines, which had worn their way fifty or sixty feet into the slope. At longer intervals were the more major ravines, also dry except for times of runoff, where the descent deepened to a hundred feet. In order to achieve a horizontal distance of a hundred yards, Stewart was required to hike, in addition to the hundred yards, at least fifty feet down and fifty feet up. He could see his breath.

Though the rain did not pound down upon him, he was enshrouded in its mist, and it ran from his head and his face and his fingers. The ground was soaking up the rain and becoming muddy and slippery, sometimes causing him to fall. There was little chance of gauging how long in time he hiked or even the time of day with the sun hidden. The cold from being wet began to penetrate Stewart's body. He realized he hadn't seen a carins for some time. Twice he walked the width of the talus, hoping to cross the route or to discover a marking. He continued north.

Stewart noticed that the wall was relinquishing its height. But he was cold and exhausted. He was beginning to lose control of his coordination, his breath was short and rapid, and a constant shiver had overtaken him. Here membered with a start of panic that he hadn't eaten that day. He looked about him for direction but grew confused and disoriented. Stewart had no choice. Where the wall and the slope merged and ceased to be an obstacle, he could see the top of the canyon, but he did not have the strength to go on. He had climbed enough so that all around him, he could see the white rim, and it looked formidable and unconquerable to him. He found a spot of dry earth where two large boulders slanted against each other. There was enough dry wood to start a small fire, but it took him some time to do so because of his severe shivering. He wished he was not alone. From where he sat under the protection of the boulders, Stewart looked out through the rain to the distant rim, which had been his goal. Even with the fire, he was not able to stop his wet body from shaking; he had sheer exhaustion. But he had no choice. Stewart stood in a shivered frenzy. For a few minutes, he washed the fire's slow flames over himself. When he stepped out from under the rocks into the wet gray to begin, again he noticed that the earth had become saturated and that the rainwater was beginning to puddle. Soon runoff would start. He was thankful he was past the ravines where rain collected to run off the talus slope into Owl Canyon.

He moved his newly inspired body north, chanting to himself as he went, in rhythm with his heavy steps, "I must not fail." He succeeded in placing himself in a trance while the rain insulted him, dripping in his face, each drop cold. He did not look ahead but kept his eyes to the muddy earth. A thousand times he repeated his injunction, "I must not fail; they will know." He spotted a shortcut route leading up and through the sheer cliff walls. Methodically, he'd have to walk until he bisected the trail he'd come in on.

Stewart was numb with cold and exhaustion when he saw the worn path ahead of him.

The sky was darkening; the sun's angle behind the thick clouds had started down. His pain was constant.

Now it was a matter of following the trail, of finding the energy for the last climb. He was proud when he stepped onto the trail, but otherwise all matter and all thoughts had left his mind to make room for complete concentration on his goal: getting out of the canyon. His mind had no room for Arthur. His chant changed when he started up the trail. "I am not a man of failure," he repeated. There were tears running down his face; he could tell by the taste of salt.

The first false summit nearly broke Stewart's spirit, but he adjusted quickly, and the second did not affect him at all; that was the way of the canyon, he thought. When he reached the rim and saw the blue truck, he realized that somewhere along the rain-soaked trail his condition had reversed; gathered strength rather than lose it. He felt strong again and knew if the truck failed to start, he'd simply continue walking until he came to help.

When the truck did start, he felt the slightest pride; he had succeeded. The matter was now in the hands of man and his machines. Arthur's first sensation after the fall and after the realization that his body was badly broken was one of absolute helplessness compounded by the lack of feeling in his body. He panicked when it occurred to him that he might be sinking toward a thick death. With Stewart gone and everything quiet and settled, Arthur watched closely but was unable to detect any sinking. Finally, he grew confident that his body weight was distributed over a sufficient area and that the mud was dense enough so that he would not be pulled under if he lay still. Serious disturbance to the mud would be disastrous for him, and yet the instinct to extricate him selffrom his helplessness was so great that he found himself wanting to thrash about in an arbitrary pursuit of freedom.

When the knowledge that his only choice was to submit to his condition succeeded in dominating him, Arthur was able to relax and wait. There was nothing he could do. When he relaxed his body, he became aware of the pain, which he took to be a good sign, but then the pain would grow so intense that he'd lapse into unconsciousness. When he'd wake, there would be the fear and the sensation of sinking again. Then panic would start anew. There were times now when he greatly regretted telling Stewart to bypass the camp. What a relief it would be to have companionship now. What a glorious sight to see and talk with another person. Especially if he was going to die. What a stupid and rotten way to die, he thought. Why had he tried to climb the face without adequate equipment, particularly when there was an easy alternative?

He realized that he knew nothing. Bitterness had always been the human emotion Arthur despised most. Now he felt bitter. He'd done nothing to deserve such torment, nor to deserve a slow and demeaning death. *And why should a man be brought from nothing to full strength only to be taken at his peak? Where was the logic or justice of that?* he cried to himself. *Where was the rest of his share?* he asked with his mind and teeth clenched. Certainly, he hadn't had a full or fair share of life or even of its time. He wanted more of life. Arthur did not really believe he would die in the mud pit until he felt the rain on his face. He could not believe that it was happening, that a miserly, cold rain had come to punish him, to mingle with his tears, when already he suffered a punishment beyond endurance and reason. He thought to himself: *To no man more than hecan bear' and understood the meaninglessness of the passage.* Despite his condition and the panic that inhabited his mind, Arthur knew well what the rain meant. The mud would lose its density, and the point would eventually come when it could support him no longer. Or perhaps runoff would start first, sending rainwater from other places, trickling at first, then gushing over the ledge above him to fill the bowl and bury him. Though he knew calmness was wisest for him, Arthur raged. His scream was bitter and frustrated and angry and a faultless cry for help. If, by chance, one of the three had happened into the canyon, Arthur would seize upon that chance. But his screams now fell away and were lost within his canyon. The pain returned, and he lost clarity. He was not certain but that his screams were inside his mind only.

Unconsciousness came from time to time and when Arthur came around the first thing he would look for was evidence of sinking or the start of runoff spilling over from above. He wished for someone to be with him. Perhaps two together could devise an escape. When he woke there, were large, heavy drops of water hitting him in the face and splattering all about him. His first thought was that the substance of the rain had changed from a mist to a hard fall but then he noticed that it dripped from the ledge; that runoff had begun. He could pivot his neck enough to see his body laying in the mud. The rain had started to pool around his waist. No longer was it soaking in. The bowl caught the rain that fell within it and now that which came from above as well. The level of the pooled water would rise, slowly at first, until it had filled the bowl and spilled over. Arthur had noticed that the lip of the bowl was several feet above his head. The mud had not loosened its hold upon him. When the plume of water over the ledge above Arthur became constant and the water level in the bowl had risen to his chest, he began a constant wail. He cursed Stewart for not bringing help. He cursed the three at the camp for not coming to his rescue. He cursed the maker of rain and mud and gravity and accidents. His scream turned to the helpless roar of a wild beast that wakes to find itself caged. It was between roars, when Arthur was gasping for breath, that he heard the alien sound of helicopter blades beating the wind. He had never heard anything so out of place as the quick, chopping vibrations of the machine. Soon he was able to see what he heard when it appeared over the inner rim like a huge and awkward bird. But this was no bird, loud and lacking grace, descending slowly and surely out of the sky to where he lay: a pilot, a doctor, a ranger, and Stewart, had everything to save him. They were dressed in yellow rain gear, even Stewart. They surveyed the situation casually, without hurry, in a professional and detached manner. Arthur said nothing. He might have been in shock from the terror of his ordeal or only semi-conscious or merely waiting, having submitted to the judgment of his rescuers. Stewart, too, was silent. He stood near the mud pit yet out of the way of the others as they worked.

None entered the bowl. They walked around it, speaking to each other in calm, lowered voices as they examined all angles of the problem. When the matter had been adequately appraised among them, they walked to the helicopter and removed their hardware. The ranger had a long, narrow pole and hooked one end. He was able to thread the rope under the mud and Arthur's body and then up to the surface, again where it could be reached by the pilot. Three ropes were passed under Arthur's body. The ropes were leaders, tied to ten-inch-wide belts of a black harness. When the belts had been pulled into place under Arthur's body, the end of each belt, three on each side with heavy-gauge steel rings, were attached to either side of the helicopter, and then the slack was pulled up. In a matter of minutes, a harness sling had been fixed tightly in place around the victim's body. The pilot took the machine up, lifting Arthur and then setting him down again on a plastic sheet-covered stretcher. The doctor took several minutes to examine Arthur before he was placed inside the waiting helicopter. After the cursory examination, the doctor said there was no damage to the spinal cord and there would be no paralysis. Stewart declined a ride back to the rim, declaring that he had to go to the three and inform them of the events. The ranger offered to go in his place, but Stewart thanked him and said he would go himself. It was almost dark, and the rain continued. Before the helicopter left, Arthur looked over to Stewart. The snakeskin hung about his neck, now caked with mud.

Arthur's grin returned. He said: "Wonders are many..."

Then he stopped and merely shook his head, still grinning. With tears in his eyes, Stewart laughed lightly and nodded that he understood. He said he would come to the hospital the next day; that he was going to return to the camp to see the three through the wet night; likely, they didn't know enough to get out of the rain. He said he would lead them on the hike out the next day, when the rain ceased.

When Stewart reached the camp where Jim, Kurt, and Martin were waiting, clearly full of misery, all three called out at once, asking: "Where have you and Arthur been, and where is Arthur?" Stewart hesitated, then said, "Arthur had an accident; did you hear the helicopter?" Kurt called out in a shocked voice, "What happened to him, why did he need a helicopter?" Stewart did not want to describe how Arthur's injury occurred. He thought Arthur should be the one to say what happened. "He fell. I'm not sure how, but we agreed that he should lay quiet until assistance could arrive. I went up to the rim and contacted the rangers and the Park Doctor and the Doctor agreed that the helicopter should be used. I was really glad about that decision. I directed the helicopter to the location; it wasn't an easy place to land and to navigate to bring Arthur into the chopper."

Jim, Kurt, and Martin wanted more information. They wanted to know more about how Arthur fell. Stewart repeated that he did not know. The three wanted to know about climbing out of the Canyon at night. Stewart took in a silent breath of air and answered, "Hiking out at night calls for good attention and following The Shadow of the Trap." There was a silence among the three hikers and then a legitimate forty-five laughter from three young men at the bottom of the Canyon as darkness was setting in.

Conversation with Vincent Yes, Vincent, it was five and a half million dollars. Dollars, not Frances. Well, New York is now the center of the art world—no, not Paris, not The Hague. At a place called Christie's, not Goupil…

I know, I know five and a half million is an unfathomable amount.

Correct, I won't argue with you… it is, what do you call it: "Obscene." Oh, ha, yes, that's just what it is, Vincent. Obscene as hell, particularly when you consider that lack of money, and therefore lack of food, cost you your health, probably your sanity, and your life as well.

What's that you're saying? A man can't live forever? Well, I know that, but no one ever called thirty-seven forever.

You didn't expect to live forever? So you don't care about the five and a half million for yourself, do you? Oh yes, I believe that; you had something more important in your life than money or the lack of it, you had your art. What's that you say… that the five and a half million is obscene because right now there are countless starving, unfulfilled artists. There are countless everything starving, I can assure you. Give it to them instead?

Do you really think, Vincent, that such an act of artistic socialism could be responsible for more great works of art? No, I'm not sure either, Vincent. Doesn't your own life offer proof to the contrary? Do you think you would have created your masterpieces if some benevolent patron had assured your comfort from the beginning? 1

You say that you never created any masterpieces? Ah, but there you are wrong, as I told you before, five and a half million—what better proof? You had a benevolent patron? I won't argue that Theo wasn't a patron and benevolent to you, but how can you, of all people, call one hundred-fifty francs a month, assuring your comfort? It was never enough; never once was it. Compare that to one thousand francs per month. Wouldn't that be much better to assure your comfort? Wouldn't that allow you to grow a little punchy around the belt? Five and a half million invested properly, say by your friend Gauguin, if he'd ever return to the stock market, could bring in quite a few one thousand Francs a month for starving, desperate artists.

… But back to our first question, Vincent, do you think you would have created all those fine works it they would have made you rich from the beginning? Maybe the works wouldn't have been just as fine, you say? You mean your works might have lacked the… excess of force…the violence in expression…the passion…but still been great works? But then how would we have known them? Oh, by the signature. I would have read Renior.

Oh, Vincent, come along, have another absinthe; don't grow melancholy on me. I can't tell you how much this conversation means to me. It's been so long since I've had a chance to talk with anyone except my characters. And though I'd love to hear someone say, "Your characters are so real, I felt that I've known them all my live. I now that isn't quite so."

Did you feel that way about your oil characters? It's not quite the same as live flesh, is it? …You know, I never really liked this absinthe; I just order it now and then because that's what you drank. Why are you laughing at me? You think it is funny that someone would want to imitate you? Yes, well, I believe it was Gauguin you were imitating when you started in on it. I'll be you never liked it either but didn't have the strength to say so to Gauguin, afraid he'd ride you about being provincial. It's not so, is it?

Who's going to pay for the absinthe? Why, you, of course, you're the one whose painting just sold for five and a half million—what bet—

Ter proof? You had a benevolent patron? I won't argue that Theo wasn't a patron to you, and benevolent as well, but how can you, of all people, call one hundred-fifty francs a month 'assuring of your comfort?' It was never enough; never once was it. Compare that to one thousand francs per month. Wouldn't that be much better to assure your comfort?

Wouldn't that allow you to grow a little punchy around the belt? Five and a half million invested properly, say By your friend Gauguin, if he'd ever return to the stock Market, he couldn't bring in quite a few thousand francs a month in income for staving, desperate artists.

…But back to our first question, Vincent, do you think you would've created all those fine works if they would have made you rich from the beginning? Maybe the works wouldn't have been just the same, but maybe they would have been just as fine, you say? You mean your works might have lacked the … excess of force … the violence in expression…the passion…

But still, been great works? But then how would we have known them? Oh, by the signature. It would have read Renior.

Oh, Vincent, come along, have another absinthe; don't grow melancholy on me. I can't tell you how much this conversation means to me. It's been so long since I've had a chance to talk with anyone except my characters. And though I'd love to hear someone say, 'Your characters are so real, I felt that I'd know them all my life.'

I know that isn't quite so. Did you feel the same as Live Flesh, is it? …You know, I never really liked this Absinthe; I just order it now and then because that's what you drank. Why are you laughing at me? You think it's funny that someone would want to imitate you? Yes, well, I believe it was Gaugun you were imitating when you started in on it. I'll bet you never liked it either but didn't have the strength to say so to Guaguin, afraid He'd ride you about being provincial. It's not so, is it? Who's going to pay for the absinthe? Why you, of course, you're the one whose painting just sold for five and a half million.

Tell me about your ear, Vincent. What do you mean you were insane, that there's nothing to tell? Come on, man, that was the sanest, more symbolic act an artist ever did. You know that. No, don't tell me you didn't know what you were doing; of course you did. Look here, look what you gave up…home, family, money, security, health, sanity, and finally your ear. Oh no, don't tell me you didn't give these things up, that you had no choice. I've heard that one before, believe me. You insist that it's true, but I fail to see how. Because what? You'll have to speak up; I don't hear so well. The doctor says it's because of my diet or the cold or something. Because you never had to make a conscious decision about any of it, Art was your life, and there was no possibility of choosing something else? But not the ear, Vincent, not the ear.

You can't tell me you had no choice about the ear. It's what I've said all along; you knew just what you were doing when you slashed that ear off… you knew clearly that the act would become the penultimate symbol of the artist giving himself up to the ungrateful, unappreciative public. You did it to show the world how corrupt all things beautiful become when money is their agent rather than knowledge and appreciation and understanding. You say again that it was the insane act of an insane man. I won't argue with you about it; it was your ear and your razor. It would be an academic question. Anyhow if you would've received the five and a half million for one of your paintings. Then you could have paid the girl her rate, and we wouldn't have these questions about why you cut your ear off because you'd still have your ear, wouldn't you? …Shall we have another absinthe?

I know, but the stuff grows on you. You're still paying, of course. We might as well keep drinking. I can't go back to work tonight. Alcohol destroys my discipline, and besides, my room is cold and this place is warm.

What do you think, my friend…Why yes, I think we are friends, at least for tonight while we sit here out of the cold to share a bit of liqueur and conversation… Do you object to my calling you friend? Oh, good, I'm glad. You know, don't you, that everyone who ever speaks your name, and that occurs quite frequently, refers to you as Vincent? Casual and informal, is it not? It once occurred to me that you might resent their presumptuousness, particularly when your experience did not always prove people to be friendly. I've thought once or twice that the world ought to be condemned to calling you Mijnheer Van Gogh and thereby denied the pleasure of treating you on a familiar basis, as it they had always been on your side. No, of course that wouldn't serve any purpose. NO, certainly I'm not serious; no I've no honest objections to people referring to you simply as Vincent…Yes, I think it's nice too…Anyhow, as I started to say, what do you think, is it possible for a true artist to go through life scorned and unrecognized as you did and to never be discovered, one time or another, one way or another? You believe it's the former, and you believe it doesn't matter?

Oh, but think of the poor artist who struggles all of his life and never is noticed and then never is vindicated, not even in death…what a tragedy. The tragedy lies in the loss to mankind and not to the artist? The tragedy occurs to the artist only when the artist, good or bad, gives up because he hasn't been recognized. There is no tragedy in an unrecognized artist whose art consumes every minute of his life? Well, that's easy for you to say…

I know, I know, I asked what you thought, but, still, be realistic… Yes, I realize that you have no need to be realistic because you're…I know there are other reasons you no longer need to be realistic…correct, that's.

Right, if the world has become so unrealistic as to spend five and a half million on one of your paintings, or any painting, then why should you make any effort at being realistic? All true, Vincent, all true, but let me tell you one thing.

I saw a painting of yours, Village of Auvers. It was the first and only original of yours I've ever seen. I know it's not your most famous, but if I had five and a half million…

If I had five and a half million, what then? You ask.

Well, first of all, I wouldn't be here. Oh, I might be here, this is not a bad place, but it was the outside cold and the inside warmth, the silence and darkness of my room, and the light and noise and conversation of this place that brought me here. If I had five and a half million, I'd have a pace in the south seas, and I could afford to have a wife, a simple woman who wouldn't really care about the money, who would be happy when I was happy… Here, here is another absinthe; this one's on me, it is I who has the five and a half million now. I'd have the money to entertain then and I'd surround myself with the most interesting and fun-loving people. Life really could be a party, you know, but this poverty drags you down and takes all the fun away. So you'll do what? You'll paint me a picture that I can sell for five and a half million? Ha, they'll think it's a fraud Vincent, they know every scrap of paper and canvas you had ever touched. You'll tell me where to find a few canvases that they've never discovered? Oh, but God, would that send shock through the art world. You say they're not very good? No matter, are they from after the time you went to Paris…Good, good, they'd be worth a fortune. I can have them? I can sell them? Then I could work the five and a half million and have a family and a home and security and wealthy friends and vacation homes and anything else I wanted?

And no more needs or wants? And no hunger or cold winters? Why are you smiling like that, why do you look at me in this way? Your face looks nothing like your self-portraits, do you know that? Are you trying to tempt me with these undiscovered canvases of yours? Ha, ha, Vincent, a good joke, a very good joke. It scares me, Cincent; let's not speak of it anymore. I don't want to know where they are. Please don't tell me. I don't want to hear anymore about them. Please, let's have another drink…I know our glasses are full and that we can't afford another…and let's talk of something else. It frightens me so to think of it and of what would happen to me. Please stop laughing at me, Vincent; it just never occurred to me in this way before.

…Oh, it feels good to breathe easy again. Thank you for stopping your laughter; it was most kind of you.

You once said you'd sell all of your canvases, past, present, and future, for the security of a meager but certain income that would be sufficient to pay for room and board and supplies…you still say that would be a good bargain, do you? Yes, yes, of course, I agree; my manuscripts could definitely be had for such a price. I wonder what kind of man would make such an offer, whether he'd be a good man or a bad man? Perhaps it is as you say, that there is no such person except for a person like Theo. But I know no Theo…

Say, we might be able to put the question of money aside, and maybe even that of recognition and fame, but what of friends? You had friends. You had other artists to look at your work and to give you their opinion and to talk about art with you and to have a drink with you and to go to the girls with. Ah, true, your friends thought you were mad. What else did they think of you? That you were too deeply involved with your art to the exclusion of all else, that you were too intense about it? But so was Seurat, did you ever say that to them? …No, I suppose I can understand why you didn't; it was different with you, everything was always different for you. Even your impressionism was different. That's where the problem was with your artist friends: you were too impressionistic for them, just like you were too everything for everyone.

You say you agree that there was something wrong, but you don't know just what it was? Well, you need to stand back in time as well as distance to see clearly. They call you one of the French masters now, along with Millet and Degas and Delacroix and Cezanne and Renior and Manet and Monet and Toulouse-Lautrec and Gauguin and all the rest that you know but I don't…But where are you going?

I'm only telling you the truth. No, it's today's truth.

Come back and sit with me a while longer; I don't wish to sit by myself. I sit by myself in my room with my pencil and paper and my Vincent Van Gogh Sunflowers print on the wall. I don't want to sit alone here…You'll come back again? When? Tuesday? Good, good, I'll meet you here Tuesday then. I should have money by Tuesday; it might even come tomorrow.

Tuesday and absinthe will be on me. What time? Shall we say seven o'clock? I try to get to sleep by ten so that I can get up with the first light to begin my work for the day…